I LOOKED INTO FELIX ZRBNY'S EYES. THEY HELD NO LIFE.

He hurled the young TV producer like a rag doll...

He held a nine-millimeter handgun aimed at my face...

Then, abruptly, he moved past me to the elevator...

I stepped into the studio...

A camera technician lay unconscious against the wall...

Behind the news desk, the news anchor, his head twisted at an impossible angle, had become BTT's latest bulletin...

Felix Zrbny had broken his neck.

THE MURDER CHANNEL

John Philpin

BANTAM BOOKS

New York Toronto London Sydney Auckland

THE MURDER CHANNEL

A Bantam Book
PUBLISHING HISTORY
Bantam paperback edition / May 2001

ISBN 0-553-58009-4

Published simultaneously in the United States and Canada

Bantam Books are published by Bantam Books, a division of Random House, Inc. Its trademark, consisting of the words "Bantam Books" and the portrayal of a rooster, is Registered in U.S. Patent and Trademark Office and in other countries. Marca Registrada. Bantam Books, 1540 Broadway, New York, New York 10036

PRINTED IN THE UNITED STATES OF AMERICA

OPM 10 9 8 7 6 5 4 3 2 1

Grateful acknowledgment is made to Christian Peet for permission to reprint his poem "True Crimes," copyright 1997 by Christian Peet.

*For M-dot-Jane, Steve the Bruce,
and Mouse the Cat*

"... I want a term expressing the mighty abstractions that incarnate themselves in all individual sufferings of man's heart, and I wish to have these abstractions presented as impersonations,—that is, as clothed with human attributes of life, and with functions pointing to flesh. Let us call them, therefore, Our Ladies of Sorrow."

—Thomas De Quincey, from
Levana and Our Ladies of Sorrow

"Smile. They judge appearances here."

—Magda Zrbny

"Trusting Celestial Seasonings Tea, the inside flap of Sleepy Time providing a fresh adage this morning: What will be, will be."

—Christian Peet, from
True Crimes

Good morning. I'm Lily Nelson, and this is Boston Trial Television Headline News. Our two lead stories this morning are the weather, as Boston braces for what old-timers call a nor'easter, and the court hearing for mass murderer Felix Zrbny. The big storm moving slowly up the coast has meteorologists reminiscing about the blizzard of seventy-eight. The judge in the Zrbny case has cloistered the proceeding. There will be no media coverage inside the courtroom, but we will be going live to the courthouse steps where, I am told, it is already snowing. . . .

CHAPTER 1

THAT JANUARY MORNING I SHOULD HAVE been stretched on the sofa in front of my wood-stove, the most recent George V. Higgins novel in my left hand, a cup of steaming coffee on the table to my right, with Max the cat ensconced on the top of the sofa reading over my shoulder, and both of us listening to Buffy Sainte-Marie.

Instead, against my will and against my very nature, I sat squeezed into a seat on a Boeing 737 descending six miles through a killer snowstorm to land at Boston's Logan Airport.

"I must be fucking nuts," I muttered.

I stuffed Higgins into my duffel bag. As much as I enjoyed his depictions of Beantown, my home for fifty years, I could not concentrate. Thoughts of meeting the Big Guy in the Sky distracted me.

I hated being pried out of my retreat in Lake Albert, Michigan. It is miles from anywhere significant. In winter, those miles seem like light-years, which is exactly what I prefer.

The woodshed was full; I had stocked the house

with books from the village bookseller, CDs from the village music shop. There was enough food to last us—Max, me, and our wintering friends, the birds—three months if necessary (and a bit longer if Max devoured any of our guests).

My only concession to human contact was a promise to Buck Semple, our village police chief, that I would meet him for lunch once a month at the Lake Albert Diner. The food was deep fried and artery clogging. John Prine, Kinky Friedman, and Waylon Jennings took turns ricocheting off the aluminum and Formica surfaces. Locals crowded in at noon and added to the dull roar, exchanging stories about their ice-fishing exploits.

While others, Buck included, complained of cabin fever or the more fashionable "seasonal affective disorder," I relished my solitude.

It was Ray Bolton—my oldest friend, my daughter Lane's godfather, and the Boston police detective who had handed me my first homicide case twenty-five years earlier—who persuaded me to board the plane to Boston. He sent a fax asking me to attend a court hearing. The district attorney's office would pay my fee and expenses, he wrote. All I had to do was observe and advise.

I fired back a fax: "Observe who?"

Bolton responded: "Felix Zrbny."

The name meant nothing to me. I assumed that Zrbny was a bad actor, wondered briefly if I should recognize the name, then made arrangements to head east.

Nine years earlier, I had closed my Beacon Street practice in forensic psychiatry, retired from the business of reconstructing murders and developing personality profiles from the traces of self that killers invariably leave at crime scenes, and had run for the woods. I had not been in Boston since, although my retirement ended abruptly after five years in hiding when Lane, a homicide detective with the New York City Police Department, dumped a case in my lap. I pissed and moaned about it, but quickly realized that I had not lost my taste for the chase.

Since then, I have been selective about the cases I work, refusing even to consider a dozen or more requests a year, but occasionally getting hooked when a particularly challenging series of homicides washes ashore at Lake Albert.

I have never refused a request from Ray Bolton, and he has always been there when I need a favor. He respected my privacy, and knew that when winter settled on Michigan, I made like a bear and lived off my fat. For him to drag me from my cave in January meant that he had serious concerns about the gentleman with the vowel-deficient last name.

As the plane descended in its final approach to Logan, I glanced out the window. I hoped that our pilot had better visibility than the whiteout that greeted me. I stared down, expecting to catch a glimpse of black water or the airport's infamous seawall. I saw neither. The plane touched down, skidded a few times, then made its turn to the terminal. I still could not see a damn thing.

My sensory deprivation ended when I stepped into the waiting area and surveyed the milling crowd. Those with destinations forged ahead. A small army of greeters craned necks in search of relatives and friends. Bolton stood to one side, a nattily attired, six-foot, gray-haired African-American. Behind Bolton a dozen uniformed cops restrained a surging gaggle of media representatives wielding minicams and microphones.

"I didn't see any famous faces on the plane," I told Bolton as we shook hands.

"There was a leak," he said. "We're going out through a downstairs corridor. A couple of airport cops will escort us."

"What's the big deal?"

"No legal proceeding in years has received the media attention this one's getting. They can't get into the courtroom, so they're hanging everywhere else. Wendy Pouldice had a reporter banging on my door at ten last night."

"The talking face-lift? I remember her well."

"Pouldice doesn't talk much anymore. Occasionally she'll do an exclusive interview, but she owns Boston Trial Television. They're a tabloid imitation of Court TV. BTT is her baby. She also owns controlling interest in a couple of radio stations and a magazine. She knew you were arriving this morning."

I scanned the crowd. "Ms. Pouldice didn't join the horde to greet me."

"See the big guy with muscles on his muscles?"

"Looks like Jesse Ventura."

"Donald Braverman. He works for Pouldice."

"Why didn't she send him to bang on your door?"

"She knows better."

"Mean-looking prick," I muttered.

"He's got a rap sheet. Did a year in Concord on a weapons charge."

I watched Braverman head for the ramp that led out of the gate area. "Why don't I remember Felix Zrbny?"

Before Bolton could respond, two airport police officers arrived and directed us to a stairwell, then led us through a corridor that ended in a maintenance area. We waited as one of the officers listened to the chatter on a handheld radio.

After several minutes, the cop pushed open a door. "To the left," he said.

We stepped into the blowing snow and walked to a waiting unmarked cruiser. The driver wore a Massachusetts State Police uniform.

"All the agencies in on this one?" I asked as I slipped into the back seat.

"We've never had to deal with a situation like this," Bolton said, sliding in beside the trooper. "Fifteen years ago Felix Zrbny went on a killing spree. He was a kid, fourteen years old. The laws were different then. The case remained in juvenile court. Zrbny ended up in a mental health facility. At age twenty-one he was eligible to apply for release. He never did. At age twenty-five, according to the original court order, the Commonwealth surrendered legal custody, but the case had fallen through the cracks and Zrbny never complained. That was four years ago. Now he wants out."

"And nobody wants him out," I said.

Bolton nodded. "Zrbny's therapist will testify that his patient considers the last fifteen years an interruption and is a high risk to kill again. Zrbny also intends to become a celebrity. He's the one who is keeping the media pot stirred."

"He said all this?"

"To his shrink. Zrbny has talked with Wendy Pouldice, but we'll never know what that was about."

"If I remember right, the only way you can keep him locked up now is to prove that he represents an imminent threat to himself or others. The criteria are the same as those in a civil commitment procedure with the Commonwealth as complainant."

"Our representative from the attorney general's office is May Langston. She's convinced that Zrbny is a threat to kill again. She doesn't think she can persuade the court of that. The judge is David Devaine."

I turned my attention to the East Boston traffic speeding toward Sumner Tunnel, undeterred by the snow. Another half inch of the white stuff and they would pay for their haste.

I had testified in Judge Devaine's courtroom in the 1970s. For Devaine, an unpleasant little man with a hooked nose, the disposition of a pit bull terrier, and a high appellate reversal rate, the legal forum was not the Commonwealth's. It was his own personal turf.

On a summer morning twenty years earlier, I sat at the rear of the courtroom reading *The Boston Globe*. Devaine entered from a side door, scurried to his elevated seat, shuffled papers, then peered over his half glasses.

"*Commonwealth v. Hastings*," the prosecutor said.

"I know what case it is," Devaine snapped, then pointed at me. "Is he going to testify?"

"Your honor, this is Dr. Lucas Frank—"

"I know who he is. Do you intend to call him during this proceeding?"

"We asked Dr. Frank—"

His finger still aimed at me, Devaine said, "Sit outside until you are called."

I folded my newspaper, stood, and hesitated as the prosecutor explained my presence. "The

Commonwealth has asked Dr. Frank to observe Mr. Hastings's testimony."

"Get out of my courtroom," Devaine told me.

I made my exit, followed in five minutes by a deputy prosecutor. "The judge ruled that Hastings's testimony would influence yours," she said.

I chuckled. "That was the idea, that part of my assessment of Hastings would be based on his demeanor here."

"Devaine's in a rotten mood."

"Not enough bran this morning," I said. "It's immaterial to me whether I get paid to read the *Globe* out here or in there. You, however, may be losing significant testimony."

"Devaine doesn't like female prosecutors," she said.

I wondered how many of a judge's rulings were influenced by her or his idiosyncracies.

Now, as we entered the tunnel, I warned Bolton, "Zrbny will walk."

"Because of Devaine?"

"He won't help. Who else will testify?"

Bolton gave me a file folder. I skimmed a witness list, then flipped to a police summary dated August 1984.

"First cop on the scene was named Waycross," I said. "There was a victim with that name."

Bolton sighed. "Neville Waycross was a young homicide detective, one of my people. The victim was his wife. They'd been married six months."

"He found his wife?"

Bolton nodded. "Zrbny had cut her throat."

"Jesus," I muttered, and gazed at the tunnel's beige walls.

Waycross struggled with alcoholism for two years, Bolton told me, landed in detox, and eventually joined the Brotherhood of the Earth in Christ, an inner-city monastic group dedicated to the Bible and good works in the community.

"Ray, I'm going to need some time to study this."

"You don't have it. We're already late. Your hotel room is stocked with a complete set of the case files. I figured you'd want to go over them tonight."

I considered what Bolton had said, wondering why Zrbny would wait eight years before making noise about getting out.

"Why the fascination with the media?"

"His shrink says it started with the Simpson trial. Zrbny's quite an an expert on the case. Claims one person could not have committed the crime."

"I'm inclined to agree with him."

Bolton shot me a glance. "Later, over beers," he said. "Zrbny followed the Woodward au pair case here, and the tabloid TV shows on the JonBenet Ramsay case. He wants that kind of prime-time notoriety. Says he has a message to deliver."

"Fifteen minutes of fame doesn't cut it anymore," I said. "Why now?"

"He has incentive now," Bolton said. "A year ago, no one remembered his name."

"Suppose I agree that Zrbny shouldn't be let out. Then what? He's probably gonna walk anyway."

I looked at the back of Bolton's head and waited. My old friend watched the traffic as we made the climb from the tunnel's deepest point.

"He'll make us come after him," Bolton finally said.

I gazed out the window as we emerged from the tunnel at the expressway's north ramp and waited for a break in traffic. Despite the snow, the streets bustled with activity.

"So, we're a few days away from somebody being murdered," I said. "Maybe that woman with the Macy's bag, or the girl in the Celtics jacket. She doesn't know it yet. Maybe she won't have to know it, but she'll still be dead."

"Too existential for me," he said.

"Does Devaine hold forth in the old courthouse?"

"He refuses to give up his view of the Charles River," Bolton said as his cell phone beeped. "It's a pain for security."

The state trooper drove north, then turned onto Storrow Drive, speeding west beside the river.

When I departed Boston, I couldn't get away fast enough. At Lake Albert, I read Bolton's fax and felt an immediate rush of ambivalence laced with mild nausea. Now I watched the city of my birth—a blur of gray walls, black windows, and white streaks. I had lived most of my life here, and committed most of my sins in the city's innards. I hated the place with a passion.

Bolton switched off his phone and turned sideways in his seat. "There's a delay in transporting Zrbny. Probably the weather. How do you feel about coming home, Lucas?"

I considered his question, seeking an appropriate analogy. "Remember when we took the kids to see the circus at Boston Garden?" I asked. "You usually had complimentary tickets."

He smiled, probably remembering the jugglers, aerial artists, clowns, and acrobats.

"The circus was a chaos of crowds and foul smells shoehorned into the old Boston Garden," I said. "Your tickets invariably seated me where the elephants could shit under my nose. That's how I feel."

CHAPTER 2

I STOOD WITH MY HANDS CLASPED BEHIND my neck.

Sheriff's Deputy O'Brien strapped a wide leather belt around my waist; Deputy Finneran, stun gun in hand, stood behind me. Ben Moffatt, the ward attendant, blocked the doorway.

I gazed through the window at the snow and listened to the chain slide through the steel loops on my harness.

"Lower your right hand," O'Brien said.

He snapped a handcuff in place. I winced from the pain, but continued to watch the swirls of white.

"It's tight," Ben said.

"Lower your left, then I'll adjust them."

"He works out," Ben explained. "His wrists are big."

"He's big all over."

O'Brien adjusted the restraints. "How's that?"

"He'll be okay," Ben said.

"What about the leg shackles?" Finneran asked.

Ben laughed. "Felix is getting his day in court. He won't run on you."

"He won't run far in this snow anyway," O'Brien said. "But it's standard transport procedure. How tall are you?"

I looked down at O'Brien. Finneran attached the leg shackles.

"Felix is six foot seven in his socks," Ben said. "Two hundred and ninety pounds."

"Does he talk?"

"Only when he wants to."

"Let's get out of this fuckin' bughouse," Finneran said. "This place gives me the creeps."

We were a soft parade, a muffled procession through the halls, waiting briefly for doors to unlock in advance of our passage. Ben led the way, followed by O'Brien, me, and Finneran.

Ralph Amsden paused with his laundry cart and nodded. He was my closest friend, a wisp of a man, an inmate who lived in the basement in a storage area adjacent to the furnace only he could tend.

I have lived my entire life inside my mind, in a reality I created, a collection of images that has made survival possible.

For fifteen years, half my lifetime, the Commonwealth of Massachusetts has held me in an institution for the criminally insane. I have occupied the same room for five years. The ward is locked; my room is not. I have been a model inmate.

The view from my window has entertained me. Birds built nests in the willow tree in spring. I cranked open my window two inches in summer *and breathed air that did not taste like human waste. I watched children who walked to school beyond the walls, saw them carrying brightly colored lunch boxes and, years later, knapsacks overfilled with heavy books.*

I lived in my world and witnessed yours come of age.

I thought about what I had done, the actions that resulted in my confinement. I did not experience remorse. That issue—guilt, sadness, whatever you choose to call it—is important to the hospital staff. If I felt those things, they said, it would signify that I was changing, experiencing emotional growth, and becoming a less dangerous person. When my father died, they watched me closely for evidence of grief.

That makes no sense to me. I felt nothing then; I feel nothing now. People can mimic anything. I have watched them do it. If they do not simulate grief, if they feel it, why are they less likely to commit an act of violence?

What I did was correct. An increment in the passage of what you call real time required adjustment. A pause was necessary in the passing of people through space. The darkened screen that presents the lives we live begged for a change in contrast, and I provided that.

That I wear the label of illness is a social convenience, a zero price tag for an action that does not conform to this country's one-way, lockstep march to production, consumption, and profit. No one knows the chemical, electrical, visual, and auditory peaks and nadirs in another's mind. No one sees or feels or hears the accumulation of brain static that precedes and defines action. You salivate when the bell chimes.

I stood behind the last door that separated me from freedom and stared at the blowing snow.

"When should we expect you back?" Ben asked.

"We'll have him here in time for dinner," O'Brien said. "I'll call the ward when we're leaving the courthouse."

Ben touched my arm. "I won't be here when you return," he said. "We can talk at breakfast."

I nodded. I liked Ben as much as any gatekeeper can be liked. I did not wish to kill him.

"Are you nervous?" he asked.

I watched columns of snow rise in spirals like miniature white cyclones.

"You'll do well, Felix," he said.

Three of us stepped through the final door. I paused on the stairs and gazed at the tops of naked trees leaning with the wind. I listened to winter's howl and felt the sting of ice crystals on my face. A man can be restrained with harness and chain and still feel the rush of freedom.

Doctors have interviewed me, tested and evaluated me, peered into my eyes and ears, drawn and analyzed my blood, scanned my brain. I have found it useful to remain silent, to allow others to struggle with the mystery. I wrote it.

The problem as I see it is that I failed to complete my manuscript. A police officer intervened, and my famous final scene remained unwritten.

O'Brien opened the county van's rear doors, then followed my gaze at the accumulating inches of snow. "This rig's four-wheel-drive," he said. "You'll be back in time to shower, eat, and watch yourself on the evening news."

I stepped into the black metal box and sat on the bench. The doors slammed shut and, in seconds, the van was in motion.

I have had many years to consider confinement, how isolation peels away selves like the layers of an onion. When we are not confined to a space, we define our cages. Children crawl into cardboard boxes. Their parents creep into boxlike homes. We require limits—walls, bars, locked doors, fences—to define the parameters of our range.

If for only an instant all barriers drop away, humankind will realize their worst fear. People will be forced to see each other. They might even have to touch one another.

The clean, crisp exchange of coin for product— which is what life has become—is compromised.

And there is chaos.

. . . on the courthouse steps, Lisa, waiting for this hearing to get under way. There is a delay. We're told that it's weather-related and, as you can see, it is snowing steadily. I'd like to explain to our viewers why we're out here and not in the courtroom. Technically, this is a juvenile hearing. Felix Zrbny is twenty-nine years old now, but he was fourteen when the state committed him, so this is a continuation of that original hearing. One of his victims in 1984 was Florence Dayle. Mrs. Dayle's sister, Sue Morgan, is with us this morning. Sue, you have been outspoken on the matter of Felix Zrbny's possible release. You told one Boston newspaper that if he is set free, no one in the city will be safe. . . .

CHAPTER 3

THE COURTHOUSE STEPS WERE AS CLOGGED with humanity as the airport. This time we waded through the reporters and their hardware, and two camps of demonstrators. As I ducked microphone booms that sound technicians swung like Louisville Sluggers, I deduced from the protesters' signs that the group on my right wanted Felix Zrbny eviscerated, while those on the left demanded that he be released from his gulag.

Writers and talking heads screamed questions. Cameras recorded the lead story for the news at noon.

A woman on the right threw a snowball, narrowly missing my head. "You fucking bastard—" she screamed.

I stared at her wide, crazy eyes. She had no idea who I was or why I was there, but I was the target that allowed her to become a bleeped screech on Brokaw.

Two sheriff's deputies allowed us through the courtroom doors, then slammed them.

I looked at Bolton. "Let me guess. The media came first, followed by what is euphemistically referred to as public interest."

"Fifteen years ago Pouldice lived in the Ravenwood subdivision," Bolton said. "That's where Zrbny lived, and that's where he did his killing."

"Those people didn't know they gave a shit about this guy until Pouldice told them they did."

May Langston, the deputy attorney general handling the case, was a forty-something African-American woman dressed in a dark blue suit. "Three dead in Ravenwood," she said as she approached and eased herself into the conversation. "There's even a rock song about it . . . 'Three dead in Ravenwood, not so good.' We're behind the eight ball on this one."

Bolton completed the introductions.

"We're running late," Langston said. "There was a delay at the hospital. They're on the road now. You know what a little snow does to this city. Devaine is pissed."

"It's already a Yogi Berra kind of day," I said.

Langston gave me a quizzical look.

"Déjà vu all over again. Devaine should do something about his diet."

The courtroom is a poor choice of forum in which to decide matters of the mind and soul, but I confess to having played the game. I saw judges catch catnaps on the bench, heard defense attorneys refer to their clients by the wrong names, watched prosecutors have tantrums, and observed expert witnesses reduced on cross-examination to stuttering, muttering mindlessness.

Like nearly everything else, the legal-psychiatric industry is entertainment. We were asked to buy the "Twinkie defense," that Dan White's dietary habits explained his assassination of San Francisco mayor George Moscone—with a pause to reload—and City Supervisor Harvey Milk in 1978. Experts explain away complex chains of behavior with vague and, in most instances, unverifiable claims. The limbic lesion explanation is always a tough one. An autopsy is required to prove the existence of the lesion.

The history of broken laws and bent minds is easily traced to thirteenth-century England. Five centuries later the M'Naughton Rule became the standard at bar for *mens rea*, the state of mind that allows the formulation of intent to commit crime. Later refinements required that the test for sanity be not only cognitive—knowing the difference between right and wrong—but that the defendant also possess the capacity to conform his or her conduct to the requirements of the law.

In 1981, John W. Hinckley, Jr., attempted to assassinate President Ronald Reagan. Hinckley was found not guilty by reason of insanity and confined at St. Elizabeth's Hospital. A storm of protest quickly followed the court's decision. Post-Hinckley refinements to the laws in many states shifted the burden of responsibility. The prosecution was not required to prove defendants sane; defendants had to prove they were a few light-years away from the mother ship. Several states adopted a guilty-but-insane option; the question left at bar was where the culprit did time.

Laws affecting juveniles who commit violent offenses were quicker to change. If Felix Zrbny waged war on his neighborhood today, he would face life without parole. In some states he would be executed.

As we talked, Devaine's bailiff emerged from the judge's chambers and signaled Langston. "Five minutes," he said.

Langston held out her hands, palms up. "No Zrbny. No attorney for Zrbny."

"Five minutes," he repeated, and stepped back through the door.

"Devaine's gonna hang this delay on me," she grumbled.

Bolton excused himself, saying he would get an arrival time.

"Why is there such a rush in this case?" I asked. "Zrbny has been sitting in a hospital for fifteen years."

"There shouldn't be," Langston said. "Civil commitment procedures should have begun a long time ago. Nobody noticed until Wendy Pouldice did. Then the daytime TV crowd got militant, the Internet spilled over with misinformation, and nobody connected with the case could use a bathroom without a camera on them."

Bolton returned. "Twelve minutes."

"Jesus," Langston snapped, then turned and walked to the prosecution table.

"A fucking circus," I muttered.

The old courthouse had changed little since my last visit. The same centuries-old portraits of dour jurists blemished the walls. They were ancients who had claimed to search for truth while dispensing their singular notions of justice.

Maybe I was in the wrong business. Nothing had changed. In seventeenth-century Salem, a finger pointed was sufficient to conclude guilt until, after deprivation of liberty and livelihood, innocence was proven beyond a shadow of doubt and in accordance with the will of God. We are all witches awaiting exorcism—our days in court.

I headed for the bathroom, eager to relieve my bladder of the load it carried from Detroit. I could have used the bathroom on the plane and, with the 737 bouncing around the sky like a kid's beachball, I could have doused my shoes with a soaking they did not need. I had elected to wait.

Danny Kirkland stood at the sink. "Hey, Doc," he said, adjusting his tie in the mirror. "It's been years."

The business card Kirkland gave me identified him as a freelance journalist. He was a digger, a sleaze peddler who sold his exclusives to the highest bidder. Microcassette recorders, miniature cameras, and an array of pea-sized bugs were Kirkland's tools of trade.

"Does Bolton know you're in the building?" I asked.

"C'mon. Surely you've heard of the First Amendment."

"Surely you've heard of contempt of court."

"Easy. Slow down. I'll split. Just thought I might catch a quote in here. It's been a tight-ass day."

I pushed open the stall. Kirkland's tape recorder rested on the commode, its tiny red light glowing. I tipped it into the toilet.

"You sonofabitch," he said. "That fuckin' thing set me back five hundred bucks."

"Shouldn't have left it in a precarious position."

"You're gonna work this city like you always did," he said. "There are your rules and everyone else's rules. You watch out. Somebody's gonna take offense."

I grabbed Kirkland, spun him around, and yanked down his jacket. He had clipped another tape device to his inside pocket. I removed it.

"You want to produce the rest or should I strip you?"

"That's it," he said. "Don't fuckin' dunk it."

I did. "That's a grand," I said. "Want to go for double or nothing?"

I dragged Kirkland into the hall and led him to a side door.

"This fuckin' case stinks," he said. "You're going to find out the hard way that it ain't only Zrbny you got to worry about."

I shoved Kirkland into the alley.

THE TWO SHERIFF'S DEPUTIES SWUNG OPEN the doors for a man who was as wide as the doorway. He carried a straight staff and brushed snow from his brown wool cassock. I could not decide which of Robin Hood's friends he more resembled, Friar Tuck or Little John. His hair was thin on top, but flowed below his shoulders. His beard stopped immediately above a large wooden cross that hung on a length of rawhide.

Bolton warmly greeted the man. "It's been a long time, Neville," he said.

The gentleman I had pegged for Sherwood Forest was Bolton's former detective, Neville Waycross.

"I thought you'd want to avoid this," Bolton said.

"May slapped me with a subpoena. It wasn't necessary. I would have been here anyway."

Waycross turned and introduced himself. "You're Lucas Frank," he said. "I remember you from TV years ago. Ray talked a lot about you. He used to complain that when you nailed down a profile, you didn't tell him whether the perp would be wearing boxers or briefs."

"I figured Ray could do that when he booked the bastard," I said.

Waycross smiled. His dark, deep-set eyes added to the intensity he radiated. He was a walking power plant, ready to infuse with his energy whatever he touched.

"Ray mentioned that you were involved with the church," I said.

"Not the church. The Brotherhood of the Earth in Christ. Our mission is on the Roxbury streets. Our monastery is a storefront on Humboldt Avenue."

"I'm familiar with the area. I lived there when I was a kid, in a tenement on Wakullah Street."

"Then you were on intimate terms with some of the neighborhood's early problems. Now we've got drugs and guns, the absence of adequate work, food, and clothing, a welfare system that's a farce. Roxbury has its own secessionist group. They want to split from Boston and establish an independent city government, and there's considerable merit in their arguments. When the Brothers organized twenty years ago, they fed breakfasts to schoolkids, soup and sandwiches to the homeless. Now we dodge bullets like everyone else on the streets."

At that instant the doors exploded open, slamming one deputy to the floor. The second deputy never had a chance to draw his weapon; slugs from a Mac-10 spun him around and down.

Waycross dove for the floor. I groped for a gun I

did not have. Bullets smashed into the wall, ripping away two antique judges and chunks of plaster.

Bolton's nine was in his hand. "On the floor, Lucas," he screamed.

As I dropped to the floor, Devaine's chambers' door opened. The judge and a deputy emerged and were hit immediately. I did not see May Langston.

Bolton fired rapidly, followed by four shotgun blasts, then silence.

"Who's hit?" Bolton yelled.

"The judge and a deputy at the front," I said.

"Okay here," Waycross called.

"One officer dead, one injured at the rear," another voice snapped. "The shooter's dead."

"Outside?" Bolton asked.

"Steps are clear."

"Lucas, check the two at the front," Bolton said.

I pushed myself to my feet and glanced at the doors. Two shotgun-wielding tactical officers had ended the assault. No more than thirty seconds had passed since the courthouse erupted with gunfire. In that time, the presumed sanctity of the halls of justice had been violated, officers of the court lay dead or dying, and the rule of law had become a sick joke.

"Give me your boot gun," I told Bolton.

He handed me his .38 from an ankle holster. I walked to the front, watching the doors on both sides of the bench. May Langston sat at the prosecution table, what remained of her head resting on a legal pad.

"Langston's dead," I called.

I kneeled beside the deputy. "Where are you hit?"

"My thigh. It stings like a bastard, but I'm okay. I think the judge is dead."

I felt Devaine's neck for a pulse. The deputy was right.

"Tac get the shooter?" he asked.

I nodded, placing Bolton's .38 on the floor and cutting open the deputy's pant leg to examine his wound. There was little bleeding.

"Somebody has to radio the van," he said. "Turn them around. Send them back to the hospital."

Bolton aproached from behind. "Already took care of it, Robbie. How you doing?"

"I'll live," he said, straining to view the scene. "Jesus Christ, Ray. It's bad."

The courtroom filled with emergency medical teams and cops.

"Who's the shooter?" I asked.

"He's a member of Vigil, a militia group that has no use for the courts. The only rules they follow are their own. This one's got the V tattoo on his forearm. We expected trouble, but nothing like this. The kind of media interest we've had in this case brings the bugs out of the woodwork."

I was less than twenty-four hours away from the relative sanity of Lake Albert. I knew little about political extremists of any stripe, gun- or bomb-toting terrorists, the reality-challenged true believers who make the world a crapshoot for the rest of us. For a quarter century I described personality and behavioral characteristics and hunted the predators who matched the profiles. They are the loners among us who use their anonymity as a tool to track, torture, and cut down their prey. They approach the moment of murder with an excitement that is equaled only by our revulsion when we read about their nocturnal exploits in the morning paper. As a rule, they don't travel in packs, and they don't invade public buildings.

I sat cross-legged on the floor, inhaling the acrid stench of cordite, listening to the rescue workers' semichaotic shouting, patting Robbie's arm, and telling him he would be fine.

The deputy knew he would be fine. Maybe I was telling myself that we would all survive, while thinking what a strange and violent people we are.

. . . ran up the courthouse steps waving an automatic weapon. It was absolute chaos, Lisa. We dropped over the wall. Demonstrators, reporters from other networks, and local residents who were here out of curiosity all dove for cover. We heard automatic weapon fire. We heard return fire, and we heard what we think were four explosions. We know that a sheriff's deputy is dead. A second deputy has been injured. Ted Blais, a Vietnam veteran from Charlestown, tells us that the explosions we heard were grenades. He heard plenty of those in Quang Tri Province in the late sixties. We're going to move back from the wall, Lisa. . . .

CHAPTER 4

THE VAN ROCKED AND SKIDDED ON WHAT I
assumed was Storrow Drive. Dirt coated the single
rear window and I had no view. I did not want one.

Outside in the world everything has been thought
and said. There is nothing new, except perhaps the
shifting, ragged skyline.

Language evolves, and creates the illusion of a
metamorphosis. We acquire nouns or change nouns
into verbs, and the world seems marvelously new,
brightly colored, glistening with opportunity. I know
this because I saw it on TV. We have become adver-
tisements for ourselves. The most intimate relationships unfold in a room brightly illuminated by a
cathode ray tube.

I am a killer. I have no other identity. My formal
education ended after grade eight. There will be no
careers for me in web site design, investments, land
development.

I have no illusions about freedom. When it arrives, I expect the experience to be fleeting—a few
days, a week. I want no more time than that.

I have business that I must attend to, an ending to write. I do not want to be among you any longer than is necessary.

You watch TV and become enraged. You have lost any ability you might have had to know that this is entertainment. Hundreds were blown to pieces in Oklahoma. Schoolkids were massacred in Colorado. Pipe bombs exploded in Georgia. You were riveted to the images. You refused to pull yourself from the colors and sounds of slaughter or soft drink commercials. You wept and screamed and were titillated.

At the end of one hour or four, you pressed a button on your remote.

You talk about the horror. You dial the phone. You surf the Internet seeking chat. Whether you examine crimes of fiction or crimes of fact, everyone has an opinion, none of them humble, and all of you miss the point.

Those who gaze into the eyes of God continue to kneel before the altar. No one has turned away from the Lord and become licentious, lustful, homicidal. Each of us holds our seeds of destruction, and each of us decides whether to tend the garden.

I expect my crop to flourish. I am honest. You are not.

Why do some of us prowl the city carrying instruments of death, while others sit at home watching the evening news? Why do some become accountants, and others pilots?

You take great pride in conquering disease, then

new maladies come along, strains of virus that are resistant to all medication.

You piss into the wind and saturate your shirt.

If my weapon of choice is a firearm, you blame the gun, and petition to disarm the nation. You install metal detectors in public buildings and call it prevention, mindless that the fertilizer and diesel fuel that shattered Oklahoma City contained no metal parts and were not brought into the federal building.

After Columbine High School the President ordered an investigation of how violence is sold to children, as if a phantom industry makes its profits by enticing kids to engage in repetitive acts of destruction. The President's wife asked, "What kind of values are we promoting when a child can walk into a store and find video games where you win based on how many people you can kill or how many places you can blow up?"

Thousands of years ago a monkey threw a rock at another monkey and war was born. War games quickly followed.

This country and this world are defined by wars. We killed Native Americans. Perhaps the graphics were not as good as they are today, but John Wayne killed Indians with impunity. The President played his virtual games with real cruise missiles that whispered into Baghdad, and bombs that dropped silently on Belgrade.

You believe that slapping tablets of the Ten

Commandments in your schools and other public buildings will stop the killing that happens there. If I had stepped from my house on that hot August morning fifteen years ago and seen Thou Shalt Not Kill writ large in neon across the heavens, it would not have deterred me. I might have taken a moment to enjoy the color, so out of place in the dismal Boston sky, but I would have hesitated no longer than that.

You search for the reasons behind violence, when what you seek is inside, in your soul, in the essence of your being.

You are religious, but you are not spiritual.

You are a strange people.

When I killed, I was young and impatient. I tried to consummate my drama in a single afternoon. There was no terror, no sense of impending doom, no commercial message, and I left my mission undone. Nearly everyone had forgotten me.

I know that what I will do is wrong, so I have passed the first test of sanity. I am not driven by an irresistible impulse. I could conform my behavior to the requirements of the law.

I choose not to.

The county van swerved violently to the left, then the right.

O'Brien drove. Finneran cursed.

The van heeled wildly and landed on its side, sliding, metal crunching metal, glass shattering. I hit the back wall, the floor, settled on a side wall, and watched my blood drip onto the chipped black paint.

The doors sprung open in the collision. I rolled to my knees and scrambled to the rear through billowing black smoke. I crawled through the opening onto the snow, where flames licked at the vehicle's chassis.

I crawled through the snow in my shackles. At the front of the overturned vehicle, I pulled myself up and slid to the passenger-side door. It was jammed. I spun around to a sitting position, raised my legs, and brought them down hard, the leg irons splintering the window. A second blow shattered enough of the glass so that I could lower myself into the smoke-filled cab.

Finneran's keys were hooked to his belt. I slipped easily out of the handcuffs and harness, then doubled over in the cramped space to unlock the leg chains. Flames appeared under the dash.

O'Brien was dead, crushed when his side of the van collapsed inward.

Finneran was unconscious. I unsnapped his seat belt and shoved him through the broken window onto the side of the van. I grabbed a shotgun from its rack, tossed it out, then pulled myself through the jagged space.

Cars passed. One stopped on the opposite side of the drive. A woman got out and stood in the road slush holding a cell phone.

I threw Finneran over my shoulder and carried him along the roadside, placing him in the snow.

More traffic passed, a few drivers craning their necks, most paying closer attention to the slick road. The woman across the highway talked into her phone. I wondered if she had called 911 or a news hotline.

Flames swept the county van. Thirty yards away, where I stood in the snow and biting wind, I felt the heat. Then the vehicle lifted with a roar and shuddered. Fragments of steel shot like bottle rockets into the sky.

Finneran moaned. I grabbed his nine-millimeter handgun and an extra clip, removed the money from his wallet, glanced a final time at the roadway, and ran through the snow beside the river.

Freedom had arrived sooner than I expected. I wore no shackles, waited for no one to unlock doors. I ran through the cold, wet, winter air.

Then I stopped running.

Chance determined my sweet liberty. No one freed me. No person assisted me.

I was free to run for only one reason.

I gazed at the gray skyline, much of it hidden in the the snow. To someone standing in a lighted window across the drive, I was obscured, a blurred figure inside a blowing white cloud.

At the hospital the doctors and their aides agreed that I lacked the capacity for empathy, that I had zero ability to comprehend the impact of my behav-

ior on others, especially *my victims and their families. The experts were wrong. I knew exactly what I was doing. I knew that others would experience fear and sadness and loathing. I did comprehend. I did not care.*

I know what I am doing now, and I am the only one who knows.

I turned and slowly retraced my steps.

The woman stood by her car gesturing and chattering into her phone.

Finneran moved his arm.

I waited until the woman watched me, then I aimed the gun at Finneran's head, stared at the woman, and squeezed the trigger twice.

The shroud of snowfall muffled the sound.

The woman dove into her car.

I did not look down at the deputy.

. . . all we know right now is that the Suffolk County van transporting Felix Zrbny was involved in a weather-related accident. Those are not my words. We got that from a deputy sheriff. We were told earlier, before this place erupted in gunfire, that there was a delay in transporting the prisoner. I have to wonder, Lisa, if the authorities knew about the accident and witheld that information. This now from inside the court. The Honorable David Devaine is dead. The respected jurist stepped from his office into a hailstorm of gunfire and was brutally cut down. Judge Devaine will be remembered as . . .

CHAPTER 5

I SLID MY PLASTIC KEY-CARD THROUGH THE slot, waited for the red light to switch to green, then pushed open the door.

In addition to the standard hotel decor, a dozen cardboard file boxes stood like a wall between me and the bed. I walked slowly around the edifice in search of labels, dropped my duffel, and put on my reading glasses. Each carton was numbered and bore a sticker listing its contents.

"Well, that's something," I muttered.

I felt no need to dig into the cartons. Zrbny's hearing had been forcibly postponed, and when Logan Airport reopened—twenty-four hours tops—I was headed home to Lake Albert.

But Felix Zrbny intrigued me and I had nothing else to do, so I sat at the writing desk and perused session notes, test results, case summaries, and formal reports. I made a game of guessing the theoretical orientation of the authors—Freudian, behavioral, cognitive, neo-Freudian—until I came to a report by Randy Severance, M.D., a former colleague. In 1994 the Criminal Psychiatric Unit had requested an independent psychiatric assessment. Severance interviewed Zrbny for three hours and submitted his findings. One section of the report caught my attention.

> *Patient describes auditory hallucinations (ego-syntonic) in the days prior to, and on the day of, the homicides. States that his voices are warm, comforting, female, and nondirective. He calls them "My lady of sorrow."*
>
> *Patient indicates no recurrence since his hospitalization.*

"That's a quote from something," I said.

Perhaps I was thinking of Jean Genet's *Our Lady of the Flowers* written on paper bags in a French jail cell.

Severance's conclusion was based on what he did not know:

> *Felix Zrbny must be considered dangerous because he responds to a fixed, idiosyncratic set of stimuli. We do not know what they are, nor do we know what they mean to him.*

Severance included a videotape of his session with Zrbny. I popped it into the VCR. The video was pale; the audio sucked. I considered it more evidence that we have not mastered technology. Microchips and transistors have had me by the balls for years.

Bolton had told me that Zrbny was six foot seven and nearly three hundred pounds. I imagined another Edmund Kemper, the California genius-giant who killed his grandparents when he was fifteen, spent five years in California's Atascadero State Hospital, then emerged to kill six young women, his mother, and his mother's best friend.

According to his intelligence testing, Zrbny was every bit as bright as his West Coast counterpart. He had long black hair, dark eyes, and a blank expression that curiously suggested peace with himself.

Zrbny sat rigidly erect in his chair, his hands resting on his knees.

"Reminds me of Anthony Perkins in *Psycho,*" I muttered, "only bigger."

Severance directed him through the events of that August day years earlier.

"I woke up," Zrbny told him. "My father told me my papers were on the front step. I delivered newspapers in the neighborhood that year. Then my father left for his shop. He had his own meat market. I got up, pulled on my jeans, and ate breakfast."

Zrbny's affect was as restricted as his body posture. His description of the events of that day was a tempered recitation. He was linear, strictly chronological.

An occasional question from Severance forced Zrbny from his time sequence. I watched as he reoriented himself, then continued with his tale.

"I went out to the stoop and cut the twine on my bundle of papers," Zrbny said.

"Go back for a moment," Severance interrupted. "Where did you get the knife?"

Zrbny's eyes barely moved. He was silent. His head machinery was resetting. Zrbny was brittle, always at the edge of tipping over. I watched as he bookmarked his thoughts, then answered Severance's question.

"When I finished breakfast, I did what I always did," Zrbny said. "I went to my father's knife rack, grabbed one, and took it to the stoop."

"Go ahead," Severance directed.

Again, Zrbny had to pause, find his bookmark, and proceed.

I listened to the interview and scanned police reports. One file contained only copies of police-log addenda, the summaries completed by officers days or weeks after the events they described. I have never been able to follow a crime chronology by relying on the logs. The dates are too confusing. This set documented phone calls made from Florence Dayle's home. Either the report was filed two days after she was dead, or someone had used her phone then. Waycross was similar: a clerical error, or Shannon Waycross placed a call three hours after she was dead.

"Shit," I muttered.

When Severance arrived at his questions about the afternoon, Zrbny's demeanor did not change. "Why did you leave your house that afternoon?" Severance asked.

"It was something I sensed. I knew what to do."

"You have told others that there were voices."

"My lady of sorrow," Zrbny said.

"Please tell me about her."

Zrbny said nothing.

"He's protective of his hallucinations," I said.

"What does she say?" Severance asked.

He stared straight ahead, silent.

Severance moved on. "When the detective confronted you, did you know what you had done?" he asked.

Again, Zrbny said nothing.

"You killed three people. Did you know that?"

"I am aware of what I did. Are you?"

Severance hesitated, then asked the question that I wanted him to ask. "Did the detective interrupt you, Mr. Zrbny? Were there others whom you intended to kill that afternoon?"

Zrbny leaned forward in his chair—the first time he had moved—and extended his hands, palms up. "Dr. Severance, if I wanted to kill you right here, right now, snap your neck and leave you quivering on the floor, I could. The attendants would not arrive soon enough to save you."

"You are a strong young man," Severance said without flinching.

"This guy is fucking amazing," I said, jumping to my feet and finding a different angle to watch the TV.

"When you left your house you knew what you were going to do," Severance persisted.

"Yes."

"Where did you go first?"

"That's in the records."

Severance placed his notepad on his knee. "I'd like to hear it from you."

Zrbny slid back on his chair, sat erect, and placed his hands on his knees. I imagined tumblers falling into place inside his massive head.

Edmund Kemper had been far more successful in his intimidation of former FBI profiler Robert Ressler. When his structured interview ended, Ressler rang for a guard. None answered the page. Kemper said that he could easily kill Ressler. A simple acknowledgment and redirection of the conversation as Severance had done would have neutralized this encounter. Instead, a tense, thirty-minute exchange followed with Ressler on the defensive pointing out possible repercussions for Kemper. The killer shrugged it off; he had nothing to lose. The standoff ended with the guard's arrival.

"Shannon Waycross often slept on the lounge in her backyard," Zrbny said. "Sometimes I watched her from my kitchen window. She seemed so far away from any moment, so aloof. I thought if she knew that in seconds she was going to die, and she didn't know why, she wouldn't care."

"How did that make you feel?"

The question did not compute for Zrbny.

"Mad, sad, glad, scared?" Severance asked.

Zrbny stared straight ahead.

"You felt nothing?"

"Is curiosity a feeling?"

"Jesus," I snapped. "He's the real thing."

Felix Zrbny was totally congruent with what he said. He was guarded, but he was telling the truth. Severance had to dump the idea of feelings, go with Zrbny's thoughts or get back to the voices. Join him in his crazy world.

"You entered this woman's backyard," Severance said.

Zrbny did not respond.

"Did you speak to her? Did she speak to you?"

After several moments of silence Severance said, "You walked from the Waycross residence and followed a path into the woods."

"To the clearing."

"Why did you go there?"

Zrbny gazed fixedly ahead.

"You waited," Severance said.

Again, Zrbny did not respond.

"What were your thoughts as you stood in the clearing and waited?"

"Excellent," I said.

Before I could hear Zrbny's response, someone knocked on the door.

Danny Kirkland gazed beyond me into the room. "Just what I figured," he said. "Bolton set you up with the case files."

"You are the same persistent little prick you always were," I said. "Go away."

"Did you find it yet?"

Kirkland represented everything foul about the news business. In a 1982 triple homicide he obtained a set of crime scene photographs and sold them to a tabloid. Three years later he got his hands on a profile I had completed in a serial murder case. That document showed up in the morning papers, along with my recommendations to police on how to apply pressure to the killer. It was an excellent guide for a killer on how to avoid arrest.

I sighed. "Did I find what?" I asked.

"Doc, I'm way ahead of you on this. I've been working the case for more than a year. I think I know what went down. You let me look at a couple of those files and I'll lay it out for you."

I slammed the door.

There was no mystery about what happened fifteen years earlier. For a variety of intrapsychic reasons, Felix Zrbny embarked on a killing spree. He was caught in the act and never denied what he had done. Case closed, until now.

I grabbed a file labeled "Interviews with Victims' Relatives." Susan Morgan, Florence Dayle's sister, wanted the Commonwealth to "fry the bastard." The sentiment was understandable. Gina Radshaw's parents were deeply religious, searching for some meaning in the actions they attributed more to God than to Felix Zrbny. Shannon Waycross's mother was in blame-the-cops mode. Her son-in-law, a homicide detective after all, lived three houses away from Zrbny and should have known the kid was a maniac.

More pounding on the door convinced me that Kirkland was back for another round. I was wrong.

"Zrbny's loose," Bolton said, walking in and placing two shopping bags on the table.

"He escaped?"

"The sheriff's van that was transporting him flipped on Storrow Drive. One deputy died in the crash. Zrbny dragged the other to safety before the van blew. He ran off, then he came back and shot the deputy. That was three hours ago."

I pushed away a mound of reports. "Sauerbraten?"

"With potato salad. There's a six-pack of Beck's dark in there, too."

"I can't think on an empty stomach," I said.

"All units are aware of him," Bolton continued, nodding at the window. "The forecast is for sixteen inches of that stuff, with blizzard conditions overnight. Not much is moving out there."

Bolton sighed. "Zrbny dragged the deputy out of the van and carried him to safety. He took off. Then he came back and blew the guy away. I don't get it."

I shrugged. "You guys interrupted him. He's letting you know he has killing to do."

"After fifteen years."

"Watch some of this," I said.

I rewound the Severance tape and hit Play.

"What were your thoughts as you stood in the clearing and waited?" Severance asked.

After a pause, Zrbny smiled and said, " 'Who's that walking on my bridge?' When I was very young, my sister read to me. My favorite story was The Three Billy Goats Gruff.' I pleaded with her to change the ending, so she did. The troll won. No one walked on his bridge."

"He's nuts," Bolton muttered.

"Zrbny is crazy," I said, "and he's crazy like a fox."

"He can't be both."

I switched off the tape. "Oh yes he can," I said. "He has a taste of freedom. He likes it. Zrbny is in survival mode. He'll kill when he feels like it. He has demonstrated that. I don't think he's delusional. He won't initiate a deliberated kill or series of kills until he becomes delusional."

"So, he's dangerous, but he will become a lot more dangerous, and we don't know when or why."

"You've got it," I said.

I JOGGED ALONG THE RIVERBANK.

At Boston University, I crossed a footbridge, walked through the campus, then headed for Beacon Street. The few people I saw played on toboggans or skis, threw snowballs, or stared into the blowing snow.

The time and climate of my offenses were remote. It was the year of Orwell, 1984, a scorching August day in the summer of my nightmares.

My dreams then were sick. They doused me with sweat and hammered at my head as if they wanted out. I waged war with angels and demons, struggled for balance and a way to hang on to what was left of my world, but I never escaped the slick-walled pit that hollowed itself out in my head. Always, I slid backward into the horror hole—black, hot, wet, bubbling with six- and eight-legged, armored insects—bugs from Kafka.

If anyone had asked, I would have told them about my visions, about waking and calling my sister's name, forgetting for those few moments that my sister was dead.

That August morning I thought my father would ask. He pushed open my bedroom door, stood in the light from the hall, his jeans hoisted over his ample stomach, his starched white shirt already sweat-stained from the heat.

"Felix, your papers are here," he said, then turned and walked away.

My papers—forty-two copies of the Informer that I delivered to neighbors in Ravenwood. My father expected me to jump out of bed, run to the shower, dress neatly, fill my canvas bag with Informers, and ride my bicycle through the subdivision wearing a smile.

My father always smiled. "Appearance is important," he said, because my mother had always said those words.

"Smile, Felix," she would say. "They judge appearances here."

She talked with the crackling accent of Eastern Europe. Her fragmented sentences were homilies, each one crafted to elicit compliance with her paranoia. I often wished that she had never learned to speak English.

Each morning, my father slicked back his black hair, tucked in his white, laundered shirt, and walked to the bus that would take him downtown. He stood behind the meat counter at Zrbny's Market and sawed quarter sides of beef, swung his cleaver through cartilage, and selected the proper steel blade to trim fat. By late morning his face was pink from exertion. By noon his apron and white shirt were stained crimson.

Appearance is important.

That morning, I kicked away my sheet and sat up. I was awake, feet on the floor, but the dreams had not thundered through to their finale.

The door clicked shut when my father left for the shop. I heard it from a great distance, deep in my hole where voices echoed and I could not escape.

Levana, a voice said, and I heard the echo, Levana.

I wondered why they called my sister.

Now I walked down Brookline Avenue to the Riverway and turned the corner. The once fashionable brick and brownstone buildings lining the Muddy River had been consumed by the city. I had seen the block on TV when the facades were not blackened with soot, not chipped from blowing debris and human depredation.

Snow whipped around me, biting into my face. My hands and feet were cold. As I approached the bridge on Huntington Avenue, bright green and blue and yellow light in a liquid rectangle grabbed my attention. An aquarium shop, I thought, and walked to the window to stare at the warm color. There was no sign, no offering of things to buy, and I could not see beyond the lighted fish tank.

I stepped over a low iron fence onto the walk and tried the door. It opened and I stepped inside.

I scanned the room—a ragged gray sofa, a

battered orange coffee table, the remnants of a Christmas tree. A small, slender woman stood in an archway at the back of the room, her eyes wide, her short black hair framing her narrow face.

"Please don't shoot me," she said.

"I mean you no harm," I said. "I won't hurt you. I'm cold. I want to get warm, then I'll leave."

"I go to day hospital," she said, her face vacant of expression, her wide eyes empty. "They pay for this place. Are the police chasing you?"

She had startled me. That this was not a store, that it was someone's home, startled me. This woman was a day-hospital patient, a psychiatric case. Someone considered her wiring faulty, as they did mine. I gave her an answer that I thought she would accept.

"I was in a hospital."

"You ran away."

"There was an accident."

"Why do you have that rifle?"

I had forgotten the shotgun. I had run, jogged, and walked through the city carrying the Mossberg .410.

"It was in the van that crashed," I said.

"Your head was bleeding. It's not anymore."

I touched the abrasion on my forehead. "They were transporting me to a court hearing and the van overturned."

"I'm not strong enough to make you leave. My name is Sable."

"Felix."

"Like the cat. Why did you come here?"

"I was cold. I saw the light from the fish tank. I thought this was a pet store."

She glanced at the aquarium. "It is pretty, but it's not the same as having a black, furry cat. I can't have a cat here, so they gave me fish. Fish need someone to care for them too. I have to remember to feed them. That's how I remember to take my medication. I was going to make soup. Will you let me do that? Would you like some? It's chicken noodle."

I looked at the door.

"No one comes here," she said. "Is that what you want to know? I probably shouldn't tell you that, should I? Day hospital was canceled today because of the storm. That's why I'm not there. No one is."

"I'd like some soup," I said.

"The bathroom is at the end of the hall. You can wash there. If you promise not to shoot me, I won't try to run away. I seldom meet anyone new, and I never have anyone to talk to."

The woman, Sable, was drab, gray, and plain. She wore a paint-spattered work shirt, and dark jeans. Her hair was black, trimmed close like a boy. She stood motionless in the doorway, waiting for my assurance that I would not kill her.

"I promise I won't shoot you," I said.

Sable disappeared through the arch. I followed her, found the hallway, then the small, L-shaped bathroom. There was another door opposite the kitchen.

"*Where does this go?*" *I asked.*

"*The cellar. We're supposed to put our trash out there. Cockroaches come in under the door at night. There's a clanky furnace, a long hallway that connects all the buildings . . . I don't know. I don't like to go out there. I can't read Stephen King, either. Too scary.*"

I ducked under heat pipes and stood at the bathroom mirror to examine the gash on my head. I heard Sable bang cabinets, cans, and pots.

"*Alcohol and cotton balls are in the cabinet,*" *she called.* "*I think they are.*"

I leaned the Mossberg against the wall, found the first aid supplies, and cleaned my wound. Then I applied gauze and adhesive tape.

Sable was like the young women in the general population at the criminal psych unit. She was buzzed out, probably on Prolixin or some other mind-numbing drug that creates the zombies who walk the back-ward shuffle. Like most of them, she was straightforward, perhaps too honest for her own good.

I felt a weight in my pocket and pulled out the deputy's compact but powerful nine-millimeter handgun.

Sable stood in the doorway. "*The soup is ready. When are you going to shoot someone?*"

I looked at her dark, vacant eyes, then at the black and silver weapon in my hand. I considered avoiding the truth, but saw no point in that.

"*I already did,*" *I said.*

She gazed into the hallway, scratched her head with her right hand while biting her left index finger. Finally she said, "I made two cans. I hope you're hungry. They're both chicken, but one has rice and the other has noodles."

I followed her into the small kitchen.

"I gave you the big bowl," she said. "There are crackers, and there's some cheese, but I don't know how good it is."

Sable shrugged. "My milk soured, so there's only water."

I sat opposite her at the small, Formica-topped table.

"Did you kill a nice person?"

"What difference would that make?"

She shrugged. "None, I guess. Now they must want you. They must be looking for you."

We ate in silence for several moments, then Sable said, "Do you think you're crazy? When I first knew I was crazy, it was a relief. I run away from them all the time in my head, so I know how to do it."

"Them?"

"My mother, my doctor, the social workers, my counselor."

She put down her spoon. "Felix, what is it like to kill a person? It doesn't seem real to talk to someone who killed a person, but then it does, like it's what the world has always been about. Someone dies, and someone is the killer." She stared at me, waiting for my answer.

"It doesn't feel like anything," I told her. "It just is."

Sable considered that. "Are you going to kill other people?"

"Yes," I said. "Eat your soup. What will be, will be."

She smiled. "I got that in a fortune cookie one time," she said. "I think it means that events determine themselves, and I don't believe that."

"I read it on a tea box," I told her. "Each of us decides what will be."

"You just got free and you've already decided to kill more people."

"I made that decision a long time ago," I said. "This soup is good. Have some crackers."

She stared at the box of Triscuits. "Funny. They don't put fortunes on cracker boxes."

. . . at the scene of the crash. As you can see behind me, the van exploded. The smell of burning gasoline permeates the air, Lisa. There is debris everywhere. The police have closed the road to traffic. This woman to my left, Micha Katz, was on her way to work when she witnessed the crash. She saw the van flip onto its side, and immediately got on her cell phone to call the BTT news-tip hotline. Ms. Katz will of course receive two tickets to this year's Ice Capades, and our thanks for being an alert BTT Eye on the City. Felix Zrbny emerged from the back of that vehicle. You can see what's left of it now. Zrbny rescued one of the deputies . . . we're told this man's name was Finneran, Michael Finneran . . . he was transporting the mass murderer to the hearing that probably would have resulted in a longer stay behind bars for him. We have to wonder if that's what Zrbny was thinking when he returned and pumped two shots into the deputy's head, killing him. Why did he do it? Ms. Katz, when you looked into Felix Zrbny's eyes . . .

CHAPTER 7

BOLTON AND I MOVED THE TABLE TO ACCOM-
modate two chairs.

I opened beers; he peeled back aluminum foil to expose still-steaming sauerbraten and potato salad from Jacob Wirth's. The cavernous German restaurant on Stuart Street was a favorite of mine from my college days. The nineteenth-century creaky floors, the sauerbraten and dark beer—an evening at "Jake's" was as close to Munich as I could get without a plane ticket.

"Do you have any feel for Zrbny?" Bolton asked.

"Where's the bread?"

"In the other bag."

I found the dark German rye. "Severance was certain that Zrbny experienced auditory hallucinations."

"Voices telling him what to do."

I shook my head, savoring the flavor of the beef. "More like a companion and, from what Severance was able to determine, female. Zrbny's mother died when he was ten. His sister Levana disappeared two years later."

"That wasn't my case, but I remember it. The kid was graduating high school, already accepted at college. Missing Persons wrote it off as a runaway. I figured she was abducted and murdered, but we had nothing to go on."

"So what was Zrbny's perception?" I asked rhetorically. "All the women in his world abandoned him. He was left with a depressed butcher-father who didn't know he had a son. Zrbny retreated inside his head and got his solace from his fantasies and his voices."

"Until something set him in motion."

"Consider the three killings," I said, warming to my subject. "According to the reports, Zrbny watched Shannon Waycross from his kitchen window. What did he see?"

"Shannon was a beautiful young woman . . . long black hair, olive complexion, a dancer's physique."

"She was catching the sun in the privacy of her backyard. The temptation is to consider Zrbny's behavior sexually motivated. That's what the textbooks say. I don't think so."

"What then?"

"You gonna eat that sauerkraut?"

Bolton pushed the container to me.

"That's one of the questions we have to answer. The second victim was Gina Radshaw. Her photograph was on the front page of the newspapers Zrbny delivered that morning. They attended the same school. She was a lifeguard at the community swimming pool in his neighborhood."

"He had plenty of opportunity to see her."

"Same with Florence Dayle. He delivered her newspaper. Her backyard was also visible from Zrbny's kitchen window. These three women—one in her twenties, one in her teens, one in her forties—were visually available to him."

"Knockwurst?" Bolton asked.

"Did you get mustard?"

"Horseradish. It's in the bag."

I grabbed two slices of rye, split the sausage, and slathered it with horseradish mustard.

"Do you realize we're having sauerbraten and knockwurst?" Bolton asked.

"I bought stock in a cardiology practice," I said.

"What Zrbny sees doesn't fire up sexual fantasies," Bolton said.

"The projective testing, the clinical notes, the reports, the behavioral history . . . nothing hints at sexual pathology. The victims' visual availability triggered something, but what?"

"He had contact with Florence Dayle. He collected the newspaper money every week."

"Waycross didn't take the paper. Radshaw didn't live in Ravenwood. It's something in Zrbny's head. We need to know what it is and what it means. For fifteen years he played games with the shrinks.

Only Severance had a notion about what makes Zrbny tick. What was he like when you brought him in?"

Bolton leaned away from the table. "I stayed with him until Social Services arrived. We sat in a small area off the cafeteria. He was shivering. I asked him if he wanted a blanket. He said he did, so I grabbed a shock blanket from the emergency locker and wrapped it around his shoulders. Then he told me his name. He was polite, spoke softly. The blood all over him was the only indication that he'd just killed three people. I had twenty minutes with him. I wouldn't call it conversation. It was more like him talking to himself, mostly about his sister."

"You said he's talked to Wendy Pouldice."

"Hospital records show that she visited on nine occasions in the last year and a half. There were also phone calls. We don't know how many."

"Why Pouldice?"

Bolton shrugged. "He wants to tell his story. She wants to broadcast it. I had hoped you could talk with Ross Kelly, the psychologist who's been seeing Zrbny for the last three years. Kelly's stuck in D.C. The Northeast Corridor is under a white blanket."

"I skimmed Kelly's report."

"Kelly says that Zrbny knows the difference between right and wrong, but makes decisions based on his own thinking, regardless of the law."

"I agree. He also doesn't experience emotion as we know it." I got up and started pacing the room.

"He doesn't laugh, or cry, or get angry?" Bolton asked.

"No, and he doesn't know fear."

"So there's no reason for him to not do whatever he wants," he said, then realized what his observation meant. "He has no controls."

"No one knows what sets him in motion," I said. "When he acts, he has no concern about the impact of his behavior. He said he was interrupted fifteen years ago. I'm convinced that if Waycross hadn't stumbled onto him, others would have died. We don't know who. We do know he doesn't like to be interrupted."

"We have a unit sitting in Ravenwood," Bolton said. "He doesn't know the city anymore. The last time he was on the streets, he was fourteen years old. Maybe he'll go back to what was familiar."

"Needle in a haystack," I said. "We are fortunate that he's an unusually large needle with a distinctive appearance who is running around the city carrying a three-foot-long shotgun. Ray, I want to see Zrbny's house."

Conference rooms filled with self-styled sleuths do not catch killers. The senior sleuth—or presenter—elicits comments from her or his minions. These observations must coincide with the supersleuth's view of the crime, or the contributor receives no nod of approval. Participants depart with the illusion of consensus, then wait for a traffic cop to nail their serial killer for a taillight violation.

If you expect to catch the bastard, you must carve out a space for him in your mind. Then allow that compartment to fill with him—his words, his smell, the residue of his actions. Get off your ass and climb into his world. When you can see his existence through his mind filters, you might have a 10 percent chance of getting to him.

I had to feel and think like Felix Zrbny. Bolton would contend with Vigil.

"We have to go through his father's estate to get into the house," Bolton said. "Couple of downtown lawyers."

"Keep your patrol unit away from the house for a couple of hours," I said.

"Lucas . . ."

"Same rules as always. If I get nailed, I take the fall."

Bolton leaned back in his chair, his hands clasped behind his head.

"This isn't my kind of case anymore, Ray. It's a manhunt, and you've got an army of cops out there digging into snowbanks looking for Zrbny. I do this my way or I don't do it."

My last statement was a bluff and Ray knew it. We had been friends for too many years to allow me to bail out on him.

"Go ahead," he said.

"Also, I'd like to keep your thirty-eight for a while."

"Your license to carry still valid?" Bolton asked, then raised his hands. "Never mind. I don't want to know.

CHAPTER 8

I SAT ON A WINDOW SEAT AND WATCHED THE snow blow in clouds around the streetlights that had glowed all afternoon. I felt Sable's presence in the archway behind me, felt her eyes on the back of my neck.

"How long have you lived here?" I asked.

"They never release anyone before Halloween. They have too many suicides then. The patients cover themselves with bedsheets and pretend to be ghosts so no one can see them slitting their wrists. It was early November. There were still smashed pumpkins on the street. Were you in the hospital for a long time?"

The snow looped in snakelike coils, snapped into taut lines, and swept away from the light. "Fifteen years."

There was a long silence. "I don't understand," she said.

"On Ward 6 we had a computer game," I told her. "It had corridors and rooms and passages that descended level after level. At the start of the game you *select a role to play, and that determines what weapons you carry to defend yourself against the monsters you meet on your journey. On the upper levels the monsters are easily defeated, but as you travel deeper they become more formidable. I was fourteen when they put me in the hospital. I played that game hour after hour. I was alone in those dungeons. I never met a friend or ally, only beasts that wanted to destroy me. I mastered the game. The hospital staff wanted me to socialize, to participate in their groups, to talk about my problems and listen to overmedicated, dribbling psychotics talk about theirs. They said the groups were therapeutic and my game was not. They were wrong, but it didn't matter. When I won consistently, I grew bored with the tunnels and monsters, so I simply waited. Do you hear voices?"*

"They're inside my head," she said with authority. "I know that now."

"Does that make them less real?"

She did not answer. I looked at her, at the tears that streaked her face.

"Do you hear them?" she asked.

I returned my attention to the window. "Not yet. I did. I will. That's why I waited. Why are you crying?"

"I lied to my counselor."

"You told her the voices went away."

"That's why they let me live here."

"Do the voices frighten you?"

"Oh, no. I hear the most wonderful and amazing things. They tell me books to read and recipes to try. They tell me to go out more, but I haven't done that. I did see The Phantom of the Opera at the Wang Center. That was with my day group. We sat so high up, I got dizzy. I trust what I hear. They've never let me down."

She was silent again, staring at the back of my neck. Her eyes would be wide with expectation as she waited for me to tell her about the monologues in my mind. I wanted to look at her, and I did not want to. She was simple and fragile and weak and small.

She was like my sister, Levana.

"What is that building?" I asked, pointing across the Riverway and beyond the bridge at a tall concrete structure.

Sable walked to the window. "It's called the Towers. There are stores on the lower levels, kind of a mall, and some offices, then apartments or condominiums upstairs. I don't know. There's a grocery store, but it sells stuff like squid and snails, and everything is expensive. Mr. Guzman, the man who runs it, is nice, so I go there. If he's not busy, he lets me listen to his Cuban music."

"Do you like to walk in the snow?"

She nodded.

"Get your coat."

The air was cold and fresh—new air, I thought— clean to breathe. Sable wrapped her wool coat tightly around her, yanked a red toque over her ears, and pulled on knitted mittens.

"Where are we going?" she asked.

"Across the bridge to the grocery store."

"You like squid?"

We walked down the middle of the road through six inches of new-fallen snow. "I like grocery stores."

"Could you slow down? Your legs are much longer than mine."

She grabbed my arm with her mittened hand. "Do you have your gun?" she asked. "If you do, please don't shoot Mr. Guzman."

Sable accepted whatever reality was offered to her. I had invaded her home, and she clung to my arm like an old friend.

"Until today I hadn't walked in the snow for a long time," I said, staring at the lights across the bridge.

The Citgo was there, adjacent to the Towers, and beyond the gas station the glowing red neon of the Chinese restaurant. "I've seen this before," I said. "On TV. Where's the doughnut shop?"

"It closed a few weeks ago. Sometimes I walked there for coffee but now they sell tires."

An old black man pushed snow with a scoop-shovel on the Towers' esplanade. He smiled and nodded as we walked up the steps.

"I don't think it's ever gonna stop snowin'," he said.

"It makes the world quiet," I told him.

"Too quiet, if you ask me," he said with a laugh. "I ain't heard the streetcar turn onto South Huntington since this afternoon. Not much traffic down this way, no sirens, no planes goin' over. It's like everybody died and went to heaven."

We walked to the entrance, then crossed the lobby to where a lighted sign said *Guzman Delicacies*.

"The trolley squeals on the tracks when it goes around the corner," Sable said. "I always hear that, and sometimes I feel the rumble. I don't miss it tonight."

I glanced at the elevators. The Towers' offices were listed on a marquee. The residences were not.

"Is that the only way up?" I asked.

"The people who live here have different elevators at the end of that hall and around the corner," Sable said, following my gaze. "There's a buzzer system. You're not supposed to go up there. I mean, it's not like the Prudential Building. There's no place to go to look at the city. Is that what you wanted to do?"

"I want to go in here," I said, stepping through the doorway into the grocery store.

Elmo Guzman was a short, portly Cuban with a bushy black mustache. "Good afternoon, Sable," he said. "It is always a pleasure to see you."

Sable's face flushed a redder red than it had in the cold air, and she smiled. "Hello, Mr. Guzman. This is my friend Felix."

"It is a pleasure to meet you, young man. And you, Sable, how is the Spanish coming?"

"It's such a beautiful language," she said, turning to me. "Mr. Guzman has been helping me learn Spanish. I had two years in high school and I thought I'd forgotten it all, but I hadn't."

"You are an excellent student," Guzman said. "Now, what can I help you with on this snowy day?"

"A newspaper," I said.

"Those are the morning papers," he said. "The later editions haven't come in yet. With this storm, maybe they won't. I don't read the newspaper. I listen to what my customers say, and what Radio Havana says on the shortwave."

I glanced at his Grundig shortwave radio on a shelf beside a framed photograph of two smiling young Cuban soldiers. "Is that you?" I asked.

Guzman laughed. "Fidel and Che," he said. "I never met them."

"They are young in that picture."

"Most Cubans who leave the homeland say they flee the hated dictator who seized their land and buildings. Fidel took back the money they stole from the people. My son brought me here. One day I will go home. I love my country just the way it is."

"That must be a pleasant thought," Sable said.

Guzman smiled and nodded. "One day."

At that moment a man wearing a suit and carrying a briefcase walked into the store. He stamped his rubber-clad feet on Guzman's floor.

"Fuckin' snow," he said.

"Terrible out there, Mr. Britton."

"What do you know? You been out?"

"Just when I came here this morning."

"Two cigars. No late papers?"

"Not yet. The storm."

"Shit."

I watched Mr. Britton, a man who was oblivious to other humans sharing the same space. He whipped out a fold of bills to pay for his cigars.

"When you gonna get rid of that anti-American shit?" Britton asked, nodding at Guzman's photo of Fidel Castro and Che Guevara.

Guzman continued to smile. "It reminds me of home, Mr. Britton."

"They drove you out of Miami, didn't they? Your own people."

"My son wanted me to come here. There is room in America for different thinking, and there are times when too much freedom can be not a good thing."

"You, too, are a capitalist pig," Britton said.

"Pah," Guzman said, still smiling.

The two men completed their exchange, and Britton left with his cigars.

"That man doesn't see people," I said. "He might look in their direction, but he does not see them."

Guzman shook his head. "It's nothing. You get used to it. Sable, how about some music?"

She looked up at me.

I nodded.

CHAPTER 9

FINDING A FOUR-WHEEL-DRIVE RENTAL proved easier than finding Ravenwood.

The subdivision, a collection of 1950s-vintage ranch, split-, and tri-level homes, squatted on a hill. The houses were postwar crap, plywood and concrete blocks slapped together for the generation that created the baby boom. A few trees dotted the neighborhood, survivors of the toxic applications necessary to maintain the lawns like fairways. This was one of the days when it didn't matter. Eight inches of snow had fallen.

I nearly did not recognize Neville Waycross. His hair and beard were trimmed, and the cassock and staff were gone. He wore a ski parka, jeans, and workboots, and stood on the sidewalk in front of the Zrbnys' former home.

"I thought you'd start here," Waycross said.

"I don't enjoy being predictable," I said. "Have you been inside?"

"Not since the day I arrested him. May I join you?"

"Give me the tour," I said, shuffling through the snow to a door on the side of the garage.

"Doesn't the key fit the front?" Waycross asked.

"I don't have a key."

"Ray always said you didn't have much respect for procedure."

"None," I said, slipping a screwdriver between the door and jamb below the lock. "If you're uncomfortable with the role of accessory, now's the time to leave."

Waycross laughed. "Ray also told me that he gave you all the leeway you wanted."

"He's afraid I'll switch sides, become one of the bad guys," I said as the door popped open. "Are you in disguise?"

"This is something I have to do," he said.

"Did you leave the Brotherhood?" I asked.

"If I remained in the Brotherhood, I couldn't do anything about Felix Zrbny. Fifteen years ago, I interrupted him. I hated him. I wanted to kill him. I thought I was over that. Looks like I'm not."

We stepped into the garage. Dust and rust had taken their toll. Otherwise, tools were in place, the workbench was clear, circular blades for a meat slicer were labeled and hung in place.

"Mr. Zrbny never drove," Waycross said. "He used public transportation. The kids could've had a Ping-Pong table out here. Guess it never occurred to them."

"What do you remember about the family?"

"Everything," he said. "When Zrbny was ten, his mother committed suicide. She was depressed for years, in and out of hospitals. Two years after her death, Zrbny's sister vanished. She's listed as a missing person, presumed dead. Mr. Zrbny suffered a heart attack a week after his son's arrest. He died six months later."

Waycross led the way through the cellar and up the stairs into the dining room. "When his wife died, Mr. Zrbny divided his time between his meat market and her grave. Felix and his sister were pretty much on their own. They became close, inseparable really. He loved her, depended on her. One day she didn't come home."

Waycross walked to the kitchen and opened a cupboard, displaying a rack of butcher knives. "Mr. Zrbny knew how to cut beef. Everybody around here bought their meat from him. He was a proud man, a deeply religious man. He was a first-generation American. Magda, his wife, was from the old country. He loved life. She wanted to go home. The knife that's missing from the rack is the one that Felix used."

"Carbon steel blades," I said.

"The old man kept them immaculate. He sharpened them weekly."

The blades and rivets had rusted. Blackened bloodstains marred the faded wood handles.

Waycross stood at the window. "You can't see much through the snow. My yard was over there.

The fence is gone. Zrbny sat here and ate cereal, left the bowl on the table. He watched Shannon."

He was right. The blowing snow obscured the view. I saw how close the houses were, but little more.

I entered Zrbny's room, its walls decorated like any adolescent's. From one wall, Jim Morrison glared through spread fingers. On another, Pink Floyd was comfortably numb.

"There's his Escher," Waycross said, pointing at a black-and-white print on the wall. "I'm convinced that has something to do with the murders, but I don't know what. How many human figures do you count?"

M. C. Escher had created a small world of people who exist on different planes, people near enough to collide, but unaware of one another, each burdened with her or his isolation. They entered and exited through heavy wooden doors and carried baskets and trays and sacks. None of them knew of the existence of the others.

"I don't know," I answered. "A dozen?"

"It's called *Relativity*. Sometimes I count fifteen people, sometimes sixteen. I get dizzy looking at it. Dr. Kelly said that Zrbny stared at that print for hours and liked to 'disappear into the picture.' I'm not sure what he meant by that, but I have an idea."

"What did he see in there?" I muttered.

"I see loneliness," Waycross said. "It's bleak."

"What does it have to do with the killings?"

Waycross stared at the print. "I don't know. I have felt close to understanding, but then the overhead light doesn't go on. To kill someone . . . that's an emotional act. The docs say Zrbny doesn't feel a damn thing."

"We're unique in the animal kingdom," I said. "For us, murder is also an intraspecies predatory act."

I yanked open Zrbny's desk drawers.

"Homicide took boxes of his personal stuff out of here. I don't imagine there's much left."

"A few photographs, papers, a book on Escher, another on Albrecht Dürer. Smart kid."

"That's his sister," Waycross said, pointing at a faded Polaroid.

Levana Zrbny looked fifteen or sixteen, short dark hair, wide smile.

Another photo in the drawer had been clipped from a magazine and taped to a small copy of the same Escher print that was tacked on his wall. "She looks familiar," I said.

Waycross shrugged. "It's faded. Looks like a publicity photo."

"He stuck her in the middle of the people who drift past one another," I said, pocketing the photo. "Felix Zrbny had a complicated design in mind. What happened that afternoon, Neville?"

He sat on the desk playing with a pencil. "From the beginning?"

"The reports are sterile."

"I drove into Ravenwood on Ledge Road," he began, nodding at the front of the house. "One hundred yards north of here, there's a sharp curve in the road. On the left, just before the curve, there was a path through the woods. Maybe it's still there. I don't know. Neighborhood kids used it as a shortcut to the bus stop. As I entered the curve, I saw a boy, a teenager, walk out of the woods at the path. I thought he was hurt. His clothes were soaked with blood. There was blood on his face. I stopped the cruiser and ran back to the path. The kid was gone. There were blood drops on the ground, and I followed them into the woods. I thought he went that way, that he was in shock, wandering around dazed. I got as far as the clearing, thirty yards from Ledge Road, and I saw the girl's body. I checked for a pulse. It was obvious that she was dead." Waycross shook his head. "Her throat was cut."

"That was Gina Radshaw."

He nodded. "I ran to my car and radioed for backup. Then I returned to the end of the path, examined the ground, and saw that I could follow the blood drops in the other direction, into the street. I came back on Ledge Road to the Dayle residence. I didn't know who lived there. I thought it might be the kid's house. There was blood on the walk and on the porch steps. When he walked out of the house, he was carrying a large knife. It was covered with blood. I told him to put down the knife. He just stood there. He wasn't looking at me. He was smiling, staring off somewhere. I heard what I thought was a backup unit turning onto Ledge Road, so I waited."

He dropped the pencil and gazed out at the snow. "Whenever I ended my shift, I cleared with dispatch and locked my service revolver in the glove compartment. Shannon didn't like guns in the house. The whole thing happened so fast, I didn't think about my weapon. I was responding to an injured boy."

Waycross sighed. "What I thought was backup was a TV news van. I couldn't figure that out. Even if they'd been monitoring a police scanner and heard my call, they couldn't get there that fast. There was a man with a camera, and a woman, Wendy Pouldice, with a microphone. That's when I realized that I didn't have my gun. I waved them back. I was concerned about their safety. Then Zrbny charged me with the knife. I was able to disarm him and get him on the ground. Backup arrived then."

"The reports quote Zrbny saying, 'Smile. They judge appearances here.'"

"I knew he was crazy. I would have been a great defense witness."

Uniformed officers had removed Zrbny. Waycross entered Mrs. Dayle's home and found her sprawled across a basket of laundry, her throat slit.

"Bolton came in behind me. He said he would seal the Dayle scene, and told me to secure the path into the woods. There were other media people on Ledge Road by then. I found three of them in the clearing and got them out, then waited until more of our units arrived."

"When did you leave the scene?"

"It was late. After midnight. Everything was secure. The coroner and the crime scene technicians were there. The scenes were under control. I figured I'd grab a few hours' sleep, then report back in."

Waycross went home. His house was dark, he said. He expected to find Shannon in bed, but the bed had not been slept in. He searched the house and found nothing. The sound of the lawn sprinkler attracted his attention to the backyard, where he found his wife on the chaise lounge, her throat cut.

"We had a no-lawn-watering order. It didn't make sense that she'd have the sprinklers on."

Waycross stared at the snow. "After the funeral, I couldn't stay in the house. I paced. I smoked. I drank. I lived with my sister for a couple of months. She was great, but her kids got on my nerves. It must have been terrible to be around me. The doc gave me pills to relax, but they didn't work. Alcohol did the trick. I rented an apartment in Somerville and drank. Ray came by and tried to talk to me. I barely remember him being there. My lieutenant called every couple of days, wanting to know when I was coming back. I snuck in one morning to pick up my check. There wasn't any check. I'd gone through the compassionate leave, all my vacation time. I borrowed ten bucks from the dispatcher and got a bottle. The next two years are a blur. I woke up in the hospital. I'd had a slight stroke. Two of the Brothers found me on a Columbus Avenue sidewalk. I owe them my life."

Waycross paused and looked at the Escher print. "He's had all these years to prepare for freedom," he said. "I have my own copy of that print. I've stared at it for hours. Felix Zrbny is right over there by the window, but he's not. We should be able to touch him, but we can't. We don't even see him. He is so complete in his solitude of mind that we will never know him. The best we can do is to put him where he can't hurt anyone else."

I wondered whether Waycross's intention was to return Zrbny to a secure facility, or something more lethal. He stared into the distance, his eyes radiating the same intensity I had seen in the courtroom. For a moment I thought I saw rage in those eyes.

"Neville, when you were struggling with him, he said, 'Smile. They judge appearances here.' You felt that you were dealing with someone insane. Typically there is meaning in what—"

"I know what you're getting at," he interrupted. "What did Zrbny mean when he said that? My backup wasn't backup. It was a truckload of TV personnel. I swear he knew that. I think he had called the media, and he was telling me to look my best."

. . . outside Felix Zrbny's former home in Ravenwood. Two men who have a significant interest in this case are inside. Neville Waycross, the former police detective whose wife was one of Zrbny's victims, has joined Lucas Frank, the former Boston psychiatrist summoned by the Commonwealth in their aborted attempt . . .

CHAPTER 10

"ARE THERE ANY FISH IN THE RIVER?" I asked as we returned across the bridge.

"Carp. Sometimes you can see them. They look like giant goldfish except they're pale, sort of gray. The kids around here call them suckers."

Ahead, a police cruiser turned from Huntington onto South Huntington. I wrapped my hand around the gun in my pocket. The cop had not seen us.

"The kids fish for them," Sable said. "They bait their hooks with corn kernels."

"On hot days in summer," I said, "I tried to catch them. I never did. They sucked the bait off the hook."

"Did you fish here?" she asked.

"Near where I grew up."

In Ravenwood, I thought, where I was a child, and Levana and I would climb the hill to the old fort—concrete bunkers and turret gun emplacements built in the early 1900s to guard the coast against invasion. We called them dungeons—winding, interlocking, underground tunnels. It was a *subterranean maze, corridors of parallel worlds separated by walls, deep shafts, and pools of dark water.*

A tower stood to one side of what looked like a harmless open field. The building was round, constructed of chiseled, brown rectangular stones, and rose forty feet to a conical slate roof. The rotunda at the top offered an unobstructed view of the ocean.

That August morning when I forced myself awake, wearing only the jockey shorts and T-shirt I had slept in, I walked to the kitchen and retrieved one of my father's meat-carving knives, and yanked open the door and sat on the stoop beside my bound stack of newspapers. I slipped the blade under the twine, and the bundle snapped open.

A familiar face smiled at me from the bottom of the front page. The photo caption read: "Gina Radshaw is spending her summer as a lifeguard at the Ravenwood Community Pool. Then it's off to Dartmouth College for the local 1984 grad."

I passed Gina Radshaw in the halls at school. Each day for weeks I glanced at her, absorbed her image, then quickly looked away. She talked with friends, laughed with them, greeted teachers. One day I walked out of science class and saw her standing in the hall crying. I was frightened, but went to her and asked if I could help. She smelled of soap and shampoo—so clean—and, unlike the other girls, she wore a dress. It was light blue and white and fragrant like subtle, sweet-smelling flowers.

Gina did not look at me. She turned and ran from the building.

My sister Levana would have attended college in the fall of 1984. I had imagined hugging her and crying and saying goodbye to her, knowing that it was only temporary.

She would say, "It's okay, Felix. I'll be home for Thanksgiving."

Instead, my sister was dead.

I left the newspapers on the stoop and returned to the kitchen where I stood in the middle of the room, gazed around, and wondered what I was doing there. I must have wanted cereal, I thought, so I found a clean bowl, filled it with wheat flakes and milk, and sat in the breakfast nook at the rear window.

I read the cereal box; it told me to keep my life in balance. Grains, fruit, dairy products.

I looked out the window.

The unhappy Mrs. Dayle carried a laundry basket to her backyard clothesline. She placed it on the ground, clamped her hands to her lower back, looked at the sky, and shook her head.

Earlier in the month, when the city still allowed residents to water their lawns, Mrs. Dayle had come to her front door as I placed the Informer in the rack beneath her mailbox.

"I can't turn the tap," she said, wiping sweat from her forehead with her arm, "the one that controls the sprinklers."

She smelled like soured milk, and she did not speak her words. She breathed them.

"It's down cellar," she said. "I'll show you."

She led me down the stairs to a concrete room illuminated by a single, buzzing fluorescent tube. "My husband took care of these things," she said, guiding me past the furnace to a wall of pipes and circuit breakers and faucets and wood-carving tools.

"He left," she said simply.

I stared at the oddly shaped blades, each with a red-stained, numbered handle. "Those were his," she said, following my gaze. "Here's the tap."

There are many different kinds of cutting, I thought, and so many different objects to cut.

I turned the red handle and heard the surge of water through the pipes.

"Now get out," Mrs. Dayle said.

As I ate breakfast that morning, I watched her pin towels in place.

Then I walked to my bedroom, yanked on the previous day's jeans, and stared at my Escher print—the oblivious wandering people who resembled zombies—thumbtacked on the wall beside my bed.

"We turn here," Sable said, pointing at the sign for the Riverway. "Did you forget?"

"I was thinking about something."

"Will you tell me about your voices?" she asked as we turned the corner.

That morning years ago, I returned to the kitchen

window just as Mrs. Dayle picked up her empty laundry basket, held her sore back, and walked slowly to her basement door.

In the next yard, beyond a fence, Shannon Waycross sunned herself. She and her husband were new in Ravenwood that summer. They had not signed up for the Informer. Her skin was already tanned, but she coated herself with lotion, taking great care with her stomach and upper breasts, then reclined behind her sunglasses. I knew little about her, except that she was beautiful, dark, mysterious, and alone.

"I call her my lady of sorrow," I said now.

Sable shuffled through the deep snow. "Why do you call her that?" she asked.

"I read it somewhere when I was in school. There is a lady of tears, one of sighs, one of darkness. They are ladies of sorrow. I liked the passage because it contained my sister's name, Levana."

"That's a pretty name. What does it mean?"

"My parents liked the sound of it. I don't think it means anything."

"What do your ladies of sorrow talk about?"

"There's only one, but she has different sounds."

That summer day, I heard the steady beat of a drum, an intermittent whistle or pipe, the buzz of insects, and songbirds fluting in the distance. I listened to drops of moisture collect on the refrigerator's fruit crisper, then follow the condensation down the plastic panel. When the trickles merged, collided to create a torrent, I heard the roar of angry water that swept away everything in its path.

"What does she say?" Sable asked.

That day when I looked up, the sun had moved across the top of the sky. We had a scrawny maple tree that cast a slight shadow in the backyard, not enough to call shade.

"A woman lay on her stomach, her top untied, her head tucked into her folded arms. My lady of sorrow said, 'Today.' Then it echoed inside. 'Today.'"

I knew what to do.

"She said only one word?"

Sable's voice conveyed her disappointment.

"The rest was from dreams. She hasn't spoken in years. I am waiting to hear from her."

We turned onto the walk for her building, stamped the snow from our feet, and stepped down to the apartment. I returned to the window seat and watched the fish. Sable sat on the floor, her coat still tight around her.

"What happened to the woman?" she asked.

"What woman?"

"The one who was sunning herself."

"She died."

Sable was silent. She examined the backs of her hands, gazed at the fish tank, the ceiling, the door. Finally she looked at me.

"Were you sad?"

"About what?"

"When that lady died."

I stared at a small, iridescent gray fish, darting first to the bottom of the tank, then to the top.

"I don't remember," I said, thinking that I never had been able to focus on the moment when Shannon Waycross stopped breathing.

CHAPTER 11

I JOINED BOLTON AT THE INTERROGATION room's observation area. Inside, a slightly built, wiry man sat with his shaved head back, his eyes closed, his hands clasped across his stomach.

"John Jay Johnson," Bolton said. "Also known as J-Cubed. His real name is Dermott Fremont. He's Vigil's head honcho. The crew hangs out at Riddle's Bar in Jamaica Plain. Fremont runs Vigil from there, over his draft Guinness."

"He doesn't seem terribly upset to be here," I said.

"Fremont plays the game well. Twenty years ago, Charlotte, North Carolina, popped him twice for statutory rape but couldn't make either charge stick. We've had him in for assault, aggravated assault, impersonating a police officer. Six months in a county house of corrections is all the time he's done."

"Can't expect him to stay off the street longer than that," I said. "He has to make the world safe for anarchy. You headed in there?"

"I'll go through the motions with him."

"Where does Wendy Pouldice hang out these days?"

"You'll get less from her than I'll get from Fremont."

"Perhaps I can exude charm. That won't work for you."

Bolton smiled. "She bought the Towers, a complex at the end of Huntington Avenue off the Riverway. She lives on the top floor. BTT occupies the bottom three floors. She'll be in her office now."

"Waycross thinks that Zrbny called her the day of the murders."

"You'll never get it out of her," he said.

"Anything more on the shooter?"

"We've identified him—Albie Wilson. He's a small-timer from Chelsea. Witnesses on the front steps tell us a car and driver waited for Wilson. When the shotguns fired, the driver split. There may have been a second car in the alley next to the courthouse. We don't have confirmation on that."

I watched as Bolton entered the interrogation room.

Fremont's eyes were still closed when he said, "Detective Bolton, when are you going to find another aftershave lotion?"

"You tell me about the courthouse this morning," Bolton said. "I'll buy another fragrance just for you."

Bolton pulled out a chair and sat.

Fremont remained motionless. "You know I don't like court."

"That's precisely why I invited you here. The shooter was a friend of yours, Albie Wilson."

"Never heard of him. Lots of people wear the tattoo who don't have any connection with us."

"How did you know he had a tattoo?"

Fremont opened his eyes, smiled, and sat forward in the chair. "I saw it on TV."

Dermott Fremont was cocky street scum, an urban guerrilla who had traded his pipe bombs for Mac-10s when he moved north.

I turned and walked from the observation area.

WENDY POULDICE WAS WORKING THE CRIME beat for a South Shore newspaper when Antone Costa carved his way across Cape Cod. I had no involvement in the case, but Wendy called me before Costa was named as a suspect in a double murder. Two young women had vanished from a Provincetown boardinghouse where they were vacationing. Police had found their mutilated remains in an isolated area where Costa buried his drug stash.

I told Pouldice to send me the information she had, asked Bolton a few key questions, and allowed the facts to percolate.

"How do you do this?" Pouldice had asked.

No reporter asked me that question. They wanted a profile, long before that term was in vogue, and they did not care how they got it, provided its author had sufficient letters following her or his name and spoke in quotable quotes. Writers asked for *the* profile, as if there were only one to describe the vagaries of the human predator. When I explained that there were as many profiles as there were killers, and that no description was carved in stone but evolved as I acquired new information, they grew impatient. They had been sold the illusion of simplicity, and they didn't want me mucking up their ten column-inches.

Pouldice had no way of knowing that her question was the essential one, and the most difficult to answer if a profile was to have credibility. How did I arrive at my conclusions? What was the process?

"I digested the information you sent me," I told her, "then consulted the *I Ching*."

She laughed. "Cut the shit, Doc. How do you work your magic?"

I liked her immediately. For three years before we met, we talked on the phone about cases. She was with a Boston paper when Tyrell Mann threw his .44 caliber nutty at the Columbia Point Housing Project and left nine dead.

"Meet me at Jake's," she said when she called. "We'll split the tab."

Pouldice had been at Vassar, then slid down the Mass Pike to Boston University's journalism school, one of the best in the country. She had paid her dues covering DWIs and spousal assault cases in places where they were not supposed to happen—Cohasset, Hingham, Norwell.

"I'll never marry," she told me over dinner at Jacob Wirth's. "I hate kids, and I couldn't stand the same fuck night after night. That whole concept is alien to me."

When my wife Savvy and I separated, and she moved her veterinary practice to a village near Kinshasa in what was then Zaire, Wendy Pouldice was the anchor for a city news program. She called and asked me out.

"No murder," she said. "Let's just do Jake's."

In weeks, I was cooking crab curry for her in her apartment on Lime Street. It was a rebound relationship for me, a lark for her, until I could no longer tolerate her narrow view of life as a high-powered career, and she could not stand the same fuck night after night. Besides, New York was calling her. We parted amicably.

I parked on the Riverway and walked through the snow to the Towers. The Boston Trial Television directory next to the elevators did not list its owner. I found her name on the third-floor list for Pouldice Media. I signed in at the security desk and indicated my destination.

Pouldice's secretary was a pleasant young woman whose nameplate identified her as Hannah. "Do you have an appointment? Ms.

Pouldice can't be expecting you. She's downstairs in the studio preparing for the evening news. It's been quite a day."

"We're old friends," I said. "I think she might grant me five minutes."

"I doubt it," Hannah said as she punched numbers on her phone.

She talked briefly, listened, then looked up, her eyes wide with disbelief. "You must be good friends. Take the elevator down to the second floor, turn right, and go to the end of the hall to the doors marked Studio."

I thanked Hannah, followed her directions, and found myself on the set for *The BTT Evening Report with Bob Britton*. Donald Braverman sat just inside the door. At close range, Braverman's muscular bulges were more impressive. So was a significant bulge under his jacket on the left side of his chest. He did not look up from his copy of *Bawdy Boston*.

Talk about oxymorons.

Wendy Pouldice materialized from the darkness. "Lucas Frank, you haven't changed a bit."

"Bullshit," I said.

She exploded in laughter. "See?"

She'd had her cheeks jacked up, eyes tightened, hair rendered platinum, and no doubt plastered the package in place with various sprays, mists, compounds, and pastes. When she laughed, I expected her to crack.

"Last I knew, you were headed for New York," I said.

She shrugged. "That didn't work out. What can I say? The money wasn't right, the timing . . . something. Their mistake. Why did Bolton haul your ass out of the woods? Is he worried?"

Twenty years earlier there had been an unmistakable quality of desperation about Wendy Pouldice. She wanted New York; New York did not want her. Now she was the TV queen of Boston, still hungry for the edge, but far from desperate.

"You've talked to Zrbny. Does Bolton have reason to be worried?"

She smiled. "Like I said, some things don't change. You do look good, a little heavier maybe, but good. Do you still cook that marvelous curried crab? You must. Anyway, we can't talk now."

Braverman set aside his magazine and stood. It was impossible for him to be unobtrusive.

Pouldice gave me her personal card. "Nine tonight, top floor. Security will let you through. I'll show you an amazing view of the city. It's better at night, I think, especially when it's snowing."

"Wendy . . ."

"Tonight," she said, and disappeared into the set, the powerful scent of her perfume lingering in the air.

Without a word, Braverman opened the door and waited for me to leave.

On my way to the elevator, I stopped at a bathroom, kicked open the door, and stared into the mirror. Damn it, I did look heavier. I had gained weight, although I had no idea how much. The jeans expanded in size and I studiously avoided the scale. Twenty pounds? Twenty-five? My doc had alerted me to weight, smoking, and the perils of salt. The salt, curiously, had not been much of a problem. Cigarettes and I had an on-again, off-again affair. The weight gain was due to eating and cooking—two passions of mine.

My third passion, apparently, was denial.

CHAPTER 12

"NO ONE SEES ANYONE ELSE," I WHISPERED
to the window.

"What?" Sable asked.

"Britton."

Sable was silent.

"The man in Guzman's," I said.

"He was rude," she agreed.

"He didn't see us."

Her laugh was gentle. "How could anyone not see
you?" she asked.

Mr. Polowski saw me, I thought.

That August morning.

I pulled myself away from the kitchen window,
slipped my feet into the basketball shoes I left under
the kitchen table the night before, grabbed my canvas sack from the hall, and walked to the front
stoop. I folded each Informer in thirds, tucked the
right third into the left, and slowly filled the bag
with creased photographs of Gina Radshaw.

My bicycle leaned against the wall in the drive-

*way. I hooked the bag of papers over the handlebars
and pedaled along Ridge Road.*

*After only three stops, I could not keep the sweat
from streaming into my eyes, stinging, blurring my
vision.*

*"Too hot to be doing that, Felix," Mr. Polowski
called from behind the bamboo shade on his porch.
"You should be at the pool with the other kids."*

I smiled and waved.

*If I were at the community pool, Gina would be
there. She would not be pleated in my bag. Perhaps
she would save my life.*

"You've gone away again," Sable said.

"I was watching the snow."

*"What happened that day? You said it was in sum-
mer a long time ago."*

*When I delivered Mrs. Dayle's paper, she did not
come to the door.*

*I made the big curve on Ridge Road, then turned
right on Maple Street and stopped in front of
Shannon Waycross's house. I knew that she sunned
herself on the other side of the fence, but I could not
see her.*

*As I pedaled away I realized that when Gina
Radshaw finished guarding lives, she walked down
the hill from the pool on Butternut Lane, walked
from one end of Maple to the other, passed Shannon
Waycross behind her fence, then turned left on
Ridge Road, passed Mrs. Dayle who breathed her*

*words, then took the shortcut through the woods to
the bus stop.*

*For six days a week since July 1, these people
shared space on different planes.*

*My father called at noon, like he always did. "I
left tuna from when I made my lunch," he said.*

"Okay," I told him.

"You do your papers?"

"Yours is on your chair."

"It's hot."

I waited.

"Where will you be?" he asked.

"I don't know. Here."

"I'll be home at six."

*The only variation each day was what my father
left me to eat. Tuna, Swiss or cheddar, bologna,
turkey roll, salami.*

*I switched on the TV, allowed the news to unwind
itself in silence until 12:15, then turned up the volume for "Local Scene with Wendy Pouldice."*

"Today's guest is . . ."

I wanted her to say my sister's name.

". . . Levana Zrbny."

*The camera panned from Pouldice to a pile of
dirt-encrusted bones.*

*". . . guest is Leonard Portman, a man with an
unusual hobby, and he'll tell us about it when we return after . . ."*

*I wandered into the kitchen and examined the re-
frigerator's contents. Tuna in a metal bowl covered*

with waxed paper; a plastic container of iceberg lettuce; five bottles of Carling's beer; a jar of sausage and olive pasta sauce—the previous night's leftover. I sat cross-legged on the floor and felt the cool air on my face.

Now, I looked at Sable. "You don't have a TV," I said.

She shrugged. "They offered to put one here. I didn't want it."

"How do you know the world?"

"I live in the world, Felix."

I gazed at the street, the blowing snow, a police cruiser driving slowly past the building. "It's getting dark," I said.

"Is this when you kill someone?"

I studied the drifting snow, watched it fold over itself and pack against a parked car or a wall. Where there was no immovable object, it blew and tumbled from the glow of one streetlight to another.

"I have to talk to someone," I said.

"Does it have to do with that summer day?"

It was that day and more. It was an accumulation of times and places and faces all crashing together.

I pushed my hands through my hair. "My father drank Carling's and watched sitcoms," I said. "He seldom laughed. He might say, 'Levana would like this show,' or, 'Your mother would think this was racy.' He used that word, 'racy,' whenever he saw a girl in a tight sweater or short skirt."

I paused, picturing my father in his chair

watching TV. "He didn't delude himself that my sister and mother were alive. He had new relationships with them as dead people."

"I'm sorry," Sable whispered.

At night I heard him pray to his plastic Jesus and say good night to his girls. They were there in the house, their souls lingering in the air like the suffocating scent of pine that my father sprayed to mask the stench of meat fried in oil and garlic and onions. When he watched TV, sometimes he looked up, as if one of them drifted across the room and caressed his slick black hair.

"God will tuck you in, Levana," he said.

And, "We will be together again, Magda."

I doubted that my mother was looking forward to that reunion.

I looked at Sable, at her intense and caring eyes barely visible in the dim light. "I used to walk into the room and hear my father mumbling to his dead family," I said. "I wanted to tell him that I was dead. I thought maybe he would talk to me then. He seldom spoke to me. I don't think he saw me after my mother died. He gave me instructions. He asked about my day. The evening meal was a silent time, then he watched TV and talked with the dead. Sometimes for emphasis he said things twice. No one ever came back to life."

"What happened to your sister?"

Levana walked twenty yards ahead of me on Ridge Road. A white car stopped beside her, and she leaned down to the passenger window. I figured she was giving directions to the driver. Then someone yanked her from the sidewalk through the window, and the car screeched away.

"I don't know what happened to her," I said. "She vanished."

"You were very close to her."

"Our mother was dead. Our father spent the time that he wasn't at his shop, at church or in the cemetery. Levana and I promised to take care of each other."

"Then she went away, or what?"

I looked at Sable's wide dark eyes. They were like Levana's round innocent eyes, always in awe, as if she were amazed by life.

I returned my gaze to the blowing snow. "She went away," I said.

CHAPTER 13

RAY BOLTON SAT AT HIS DESK. NEVILLE Waycross leaned against the wall.

"Pouldice give you the time of day?" Bolton asked.

"Tonight," I said, pushing aside some papers and sitting on the corner of his desk. "We have a date."

Bolton's eyes widened.

"Don't worry. I'll pick up some condoms. You get anything out of Fremont?"

Bolton shook his head. "We had eight of his cronies in here. Nothing. Wilson's driver dumped the car in a parking garage downtown. The technicians are lifting prints now. Wilson has a half-brother, Nicky Noonan. A patrol unit is bringing him in. Wilson and Noonan share more than a fraternal history."

"Any leads on Zrbny?"

"Sure," Bolton said, leaning back in his chair. "He was at the kiosk in Harvard Square before the deputies picked him up at the hospital this morning. He had lunch at Durgin Park, the Union Oyster House, and a cafeteria on Park Street."

"Big guy, big appetite," I muttered.

"But nobody ever really sees him," Waycross said. "It's what I was telling you earlier, Lucas."

"I know what Neville means," Bolton said. "Fifteen years ago we interviewed kids at the school he attended. If they remembered him at all, it was as a name that took up space in the classroom. A couple of teachers said he was bright, but didn't apply himself."

"He's like a ghost," Waycross continued. "Ray, what was it the kids said about him disappearing into the hillside?"

Bolton sighed. "Just that. Kids would see him on the path through the woods. Then they wouldn't. They thought he had a cave up there. Lucas, how much time do we have?"

A parole board released Edmund Emil Kemper III from Atascadero State Hospital after he had served five years for killing his grandparents. In his confession to police, he said he shot and repeatedly stabbed his grandmother, then waited for his grandfather to come home and shot him, because he wanted to know what it felt like to kill. Three years after his release he killed again—eight times in twenty-three months.

In 1981, Michael Ross dragged an Ohio sixteen-year-old into the bushes, and bound and gagged her before police interrupted him. He pleaded guilty and was given a probationary sentence of two years. Six months later he tried to strangle a woman in her home. A month later, out on bail and undergoing a sixty-day psychiatric evaluation in Connecticut, Ross killed for the first of at least six times.

The man of two dozen aliases, and alleged killer of eight known victims, Angel Maturino Resendiz, was detained and released by the Immigration and Naturalization Service in El Paso on June 2, 1999. Days later, two of his suspected victims were found, bludgeoned to death.

"I don't know the answer to that question," I told Bolton.

"What are we paying you for?"

"To observe a man that the Commonwealth had in custody. I get time-and-a-half for schussing around Boston."

"I'd like to look at the files," Waycross said.

Bolton opened his mouth, but the former cop silenced him with a wave of his hand.

"I saw Shannon. I don't want to read about her. I've never read any of the case materials. There might be something in there that I don't know about, or that I've forgotten."

"There are copies of most of the reports in the conference room," Bolton said.

"Take time out to watch the BTT evening news," I told him as he headed for the door.

"Why do you care what Pouldice's outfit has to say?" Bolton asked.

"She's a CEO. What's she doing in the studio

prepping for a newscast hours before it airs? And why does she have her muscle with her?"

"Braverman?"

"She knows something that we don't," I said.

"BTT coverage has been nonstop since this morning. Every reported sighting, we get there, Vigil's already there and BTT's cameras are shooting the story. Pouldice's people are getting interviews before we get them. We have to stand in line. Things have gotten crazy, Lucas."

"This has always been a crazy business. You just never noticed. You ready to get out?"

Bolton had been eligible for retirement for three years. He refused to leave until he had cleared his cold cases.

"I've got one more unsolved, Stallings. When that's a wrap, I'm out of here."

I remembered the case. Theresa Stallings was fifteen, a high school freshman when she disappeared from a Dorchester basketball court.

"That was ten years ago," I said.

"Eleven last September."

"You never found a body."

"Nothing. I've got a short, red-haired guy hanging around the court a couple of days before she disappeared, and I've got a white car, no make."

"You planning to die behind that desk?"

"I still talk with Mrs. Stallings every Friday before I leave the office. She tells me how the kids are doing. Virginia is on the dean's list in college. William's wife is going to have a baby."

Bolton pushed himself from the desk and stood. "I'm tired, Lucas. I won't deny it. When Louise died, I promised myself they'd all be closed before I walked out the door. I dream about Theresa Stallings."

Ray's wife Louise died of leukemia six years earlier. Her nightmare throughout their marriage was that a police captain would knock on her door at three A.M. to tell her that she was a widow. She was certain that Ray would predecease her, and die violently, but she never asked him to stop being a cop. She hated the bad guys and loved that her husband brought them down.

"Ray, you gave me shit about getting back into it."

"You can give me shit about not getting out of it."

Bolton paced his office.

I thumbed through lead sheets. One of them caught my attention.

"Have you been through these?" I asked.

"Those are the ones that have been checked."

"An officer responded to each of these?"

"Yeah. Why?"

"This description is pretty damn good."

"It's been all over the tube."

"Near the Sears building . . . man running . . . carrying a riot gun."

"A unit went out there, there wasn't anybody. There's a fucking blizzard going on."

I had probably heard Ray Bolton swear a dozen times in twenty-five years. He was the epitome of the placid, probing detective. Felix Zrbny, the assault on the courthouse, and mention of Theresa Stallings were more than enough to crack his relaxed exterior. Inside, he was at a boil.

I walked to the window and stared at the snow. The wind was stronger, blowing from the northeast.

I turned as two detectives escorted Albie Wilson's half-brother, Nicky Noonan, to the interrogation room. A third officer brought Bolton the report he was waiting for. Technicians had identified Noonan's prints in the abandoned getaway car.

"Has he waltzed with Miranda?" Bolton asked.

"Signed a waiver of rights," a detective said.

"He have anything to say on the way in?"

"Weepy about his brother."

Bolton nodded and entered the interrogation room. I went as far as the observation area.

"Albie's dead," Noonan said immediately. "You should have some respect for the dead."

"Your brother didn't show much respect for the three people he killed."

Noonan turned away.

"We found the car," Bolton said.

"I don't know what you're talking about."

"You didn't do a very good job of wiping it down. Your prints are all over it."

Noonan spun around. "Big fucking deal. Maybe I stole a car. What's that? Six months? Probation?"

"Life," Bolton said.

"Bullshit."

"No eligibility for parole."

"You're fucking crazy," Noonan said, panic creeping into his voice.

"Accessory to homicide, three counts. The court will not look kindly on the murders of a sheriff's deputy, a prosecutor, and a judge."

Noonan fell against the back of his chair as if Bolton had slammed him with a two-by-four. "What the fuck are you talking about? This ain't right."

Bolton was silent.

"Fuck," Noonan yelled, and smacked his hand on the table.

"Who bought the kill?" Bolton asked.

Noonan tapped his fingers. "Albie never said nothing about a hit. Shoot up the place and run. Make noise. That's what he told me."

Bolton said nothing.

"I figured it was a Vigil thing. Albie was into that. I never asked, and he never said. I just figured. My piece was a grand. Boost the car, drive it, dump it. That's all. I heard the fucking cannons blasting and I got out of there."

"J-Cubed?"

"Albie knew him. I never had anything to do with those assholes." Noonan yanked back his sleeves. "Look. No fuckin' tattoos."

"Your brother's dead. You're going to do his time in Walpole."

Noonan slapped his hands on top of his head, his eyes wide. "I don't fuckin' know anything."

Bolton stood and, in a brilliant reversal, said, "You need a lawyer."

Cops never want perps to lawyer up. They ease through the Miranda warning, slide into interrogation, and hope the perp doesn't cry for his attorney. Noonan was dumb, but he had been around enough to know that Bolton would advise him to run for cover only if Bolton was certain he had Noonan nailed.

"I don't want a fuckin' lawyer," Noonan said. "I want to work this out. Right now. I can't do no life. Jesus. I stole a fuckin' car."

"You sit here and think about that," Bolton said. "Maybe I'll be back."

"Nice piece of work," I said when Bolton joined me.

"I'll let him cook for twenty minutes. He'll confess to the crucifixion after that."

I leaned back in my chair and swung my legs onto the corner of Bolton's desk. "What if Noonan's telling the truth, that it wasn't supposed to be a hit?"

"What difference does it make? We've got three dead."

I did not know if Vigil's or Albie Wilson's intent

made a damn bit of difference, but it bothered me. "What's standard security at the courthouse?" I asked.

"One officer on the doors, one beside the bench."

Wilson could not have known about the increase in personnel. He jumped from the car and ran up the steps waving his Mac-10 to scatter the crowd. Then he crashed through the doors and ran into two deputies, not one, and two shotgun-wielding tactical officers.

"You were standing on Wilson's right and you were firing at him. He didn't return fire. He shot all his rounds to his left. He even hit the fucking wall."

Bolton shook his head. "I'm not following you."

I shrugged. "I'm not sure where I'm going."

Bolton had stood twenty feet in front of Wilson and rapid-fired nine-millimeter slugs at him. Wilson had ignored him. I had no idea what that meant, but even an idiot in that situation will try to avoid getting his head blown off. Maybe Wilson was that crazy, but I wanted to find out.

"See what you can get from Noonan," I said.

"Where you gonna be?"

"Riddle's Bar. I could use a Guinness."

"Lucas, I had a call from Fran Raymond. She's one of the Zrbny estate attorneys. She saw you and Waycross on TV walking out of Zrbny's house. She was pissed. It took ten minutes to talk her out of filing a complaint."

"I'll be more careful, Ray," I said.

"Take some company to Riddle's," he added. "People have been known to come out of there bruised. A few haven't come out at all."

DANNY KIRKLAND STOOD IN THE HALLWAY. "It's a pleasure to see you get your ass in a sling," he said. "It was especially enjoyable to see it televised. I didn't have to lift a finger. For the record, how many illegal entries does this make?"

"You got something you want flushed?" I asked.

"If you weren't such a prick, we could compare notes, make life easier for both of us."

"If you weren't such a sleaze, I might believe what you had to say," I said, walking down the hall to the conference room in search of my posse, Neville Waycross.

CHAPTER 14

THE CAR SWERVED AND SKIDDED TO A HALT *thirty yards away. I gripped the gun and waited.*

A man climbed from the snow-covered Toyota and stared at me. Despite his bulky coat and stocking cap, he looked familiar. After a moment he raised his hand and waved tentatively.

"Felix? It's me, Ben Moffatt."

I waited.

Ben approached through the snow. "What are you doing? What happened? I heard there was an accident. On TV they said you killed a police officer."

"Go home, Ben," I told him.

He froze, continuing to stare at me. "I can't do that, Felix. You have to go back to the hospital. Every cop in the city is looking for you."

"Go home. Watch TV. Eat dinner."

He gazed over his shoulder at his car, then again at me. "I can't force you," he said, finally arriving at a conclusion.

I said nothing.

He shrugged helplessly. "I have to tell the police I saw you."

A powerful gust of wind churned the snow between us.

"I don't have a choice about that, Felix."

"Go home, Ben," I said again.

"Come with me right now, Felix. We can try to sort out things. You'll be safe in the hospital."

I removed the handgun from my pocket and aimed at Ben's chest. "Get in the car and drive away," I said.

It was curious. I still had no wish to kill Ben Moffatt.

He raised his arms and backed to his car. The tires spun in the snow, then grabbed, and the Toyota skidded down the Riverway.

Sable stood in her doorway. "Who was that, Felix?" she asked. "He knows you."

"I'll be back," I said, and shuffled through the drifts to the bridge.

THE OLD MAN CONTINUED TO PUSH SNOW with his scoop. "I can't keep up with it," he said.

He looked fatigued, and breathed heavily.

"Let me do some," I said. "I haven't shoveled snow in a long time."

He stepped aside and watched as I cleared a swath the length of the esplande. "You're young and *strong," he said. "You make it look easy. Where's your lady?"*

"Waiting," I said.

He nodded and lighted a cigarette. "My social security ain't enough to live on. The rest of the year, this job's okay. I cut the grass, tend the flowers. Most winters we don't get storms like this. You from around here?"

"Ravenwood."

"The old fort," he said.

"You know it?"

"I remember them taking turns up there watching for U-boats. Seemed like everybody saw one, or thought they did. I never went there. Just heard about it. After the war they built all them houses. You ever go in the dungeons? I hear some people got lost in there."

"I played in the tunnels," I said.

"Kids ain't scared of things the way grown-ups are."

I considered that. I had no memory of fear. I remembered helplessness, but I did not remember caring that there were things I could not do. Time passed, and I mastered what had seemed impossible.

I finished clearing the snow from the esplanade and moved to the first wide step. Under the most recent four inches of wet snow, the cement was cracked and permanently stained black. Bricks in the wall at the side of the stairs were chipped, some replaced with bricks of different colors.

"I thought this building was new," I said.

"Maybe ten years," the old man answered, following my gaze to the damaged wall. "Maybe eight. Places like this ain't built to live long. They've got no personality, know what I'm saying? This here's a place to eat, sleep, and make money. It's like a toy that breaks on the day after Christmas, only this takes a little longer."

"Who pays you?" I asked.

"Pouldice Media. They own the whole place. They wanted me to poison the sparrows and the pigeons, but I wouldn't do it. They don't know it, but I give seeds to the birds, and pieces of orange when I got one. I do it round the side there where nobody can see."

I pushed the scoop across the bottom step.

"I ain't got much," the old man said. "Can you use a dollar?"

I shook my head and leaned the scoop against the wall. "My name is Felix."

"Eddie," he said, and we shook hands. "You maybe just gave me a little longer to be on this earth."

I RODE THE ELEVATOR TO THE SECOND floor, turned right, and walked to the studio doors. The red On Air light was switched off.

A man sat immediately inside the doors. I showed him the card that Wendy Pouldice had given to me at the hospital. He stared at it, but said nothing.

"Is she here?" I asked.

Then the doors opened, and she walked in.

"Felix, I'm so glad you're here. I have everything arranged for us. We'll tape you for six o'clock. By eleven tonight you'll be coast-to-coast."

Pouldice was heavily made up, not at all like she looked when she visited me.

"I don't want to be a news bulletin," I said. "I want people to see me, to know my life. That's what we talked about."

"It has to start this way, Felix. Trust me. I know this business. Right now, you are news. In six months or a year, then we go with a made-for-TV docudrama."

"It's all the same," I said. "Maybe you don't know your own business. It's all entertainment, a competition for ratings and sponsors and money. There isn't any news. There is only opportunity. For fifteen years people have been asking me questions. I want to answer those questions."

I gazed at the pockets of darkness in the studio. A single light illuminated a long desk and, behind it, a mural of the Boston skyline at night. A sign on the desk front read BTT Evening News with Bob Britton.

"This is Donald Braverman," Pouldice said, indicating the man who sat holding the card I had given him. "Donald is my assistant. I think I told you about him."

He did not look up.

"Who is Britton?" I asked.

"Bob is our news anchor. He'll play the tape on his show, and he'll do the commentary."

"Does he smoke cigars?"

Her forehead creased. "Yes. Why?"

"How did you know I would come here today?"

She frowned and held out her hands, palms up. "That was our agreement, Felix."

"I said that I would come here when I was released."

"Oh, I understand. We knew about the accident, of course, and . . . the shooting. We've been covering the story all day. When I heard that you walked away from the crash, I expected you to come here."

"I don't like this."

Something about the setting and the players bothered me. Wendy Pouldice offered me the audience of millions that I wanted, but she was not the woman who touched my arm and talked slowly when we met at the hospital. What she offered now was minutes on a newscast.

"You told me that you wanted to talk about . . . that day," she said.

"There's more."

She glanced at her watch.

"Tomorrow," I said.

"Felix, a lot of things can happen between now and then."

Donald pushed himself from his chair.

"Sit down," I told him.

"I'll handle this, Donald," she said.

"I want to do this the way I've always seen it in my mind," I said.

Braverman sat down.

"Who told Eddie to poison the birds?" I asked.

"I don't know what you mean."

"Do you know Eddie?"

She looked at Braverman, who shrugged.

"I don't know Eddie," she said. "Felix, we need to decide what we're going to do."

I heard a soft whistle, then a whisper. My head hurt, and my eyes were tired.

"Something isn't right," I said.

"You're safe here," Pouldice said, her words arriving from a distance.

I pushed open the doors, a buzz in my head, a pain creeping down the back of my neck.

"Felix," Pouldice said.

I walked to the elevator.

MR. GUZMAN WAS CLOSING HIS SHOP. "FELIX,"
he called as I walked to the exit. "I remembered your name, right?"

"And you are Mr. Guzman."

He smiled. "Will you be seeing Sable tonight?"

I nodded.

He ducked into his store and emerged with a small bunch of flowers and a paper bag. "I would only have to throw these away," he said. "It's a waste."

He slipped the bag over the bouquet. "Tell her to put them in water right away."

"She will like these," I told him.

He grabbed his broom. "Good night," he said.

A SCARRED MAHOGANY BAR DIVIDED Riddle's.

On one side, a patron labored over burger and fries. The second, larger area attracted the neighborhood's serious drinkers.

Blue-gray smoke spiraled from overfilled ashtrays. Conversation was sparse and muffled, and Dennis Day crooned from the jukebox. Riddle's had ignored the passage of thirty-five years.

It is trite to say that Boston never changes, that the city's deep cultural rifts just grow deeper and molder with the passage of time. Beantown's melting pot never did have much of a flame, and no one stirred the ethnic stew. Racial, religious, and ethnic enclaves defined geography and politics. This turf happened to be owned by white, Irish-American, Roman Catholic, clean-shaven males.

Two men sat at the bar nursing whiskey shots and draft chasers. Three more occupied a table and watched a basketball game on a silent TV. J-Cubed—Dermott Fremont—sat with a newspaper, a mug of Guinness, and a young girl on his lap. The kid's age was indeterminate—twelve? fifteen?—but she had no business in Riddle's. She leaned across the table doodling on a placemat.

Behind Fremont the wall was decorated with Vigil's flag and other memorabilia, all displaying the same logo: black lightning bolts slicing through a black V on a dark blue field. The insignia resembled a bad, oddly shaped bruise.

Neville Waycross positioned himself near the bar. He had been eager to "go to work," if only in an unofficial capacity. He feigned interest in San Antonio's dismantling of the Lakers.

I walked to Fremont's table.

"My name is Lucas Frank."

He continued to read his newspaper. "You're not a cop," he said, and sipped his Guinness.

"I want to find Felix Zrbny before anyone else gets hurt."

He flipped through the *Herald* sports pages. I sat opposite him.

Fremont glanced at the bar. "Willy, show this gentleman the door."

There was a brief skirmish at the bar, followed by the sound of glass breaking and a low moan behind me. Waycross told one of the obstreperous patrons under his care to stay put.

The girl pushed away from the table, staring wide-eyed at the front of the bar.

"You're in deep shit, old man," Fremont said.

"Willy," I called. "Bring me a mug of that Guinness."

I pointed my finger at the kid. "You, child, go home."

She grabbed her coat and ran.

"Who the fuck you think you are? You're fuckin' dead meat."

"Let me remind you of your first observation, Mr. Fremont. I'm not a cop, which means that I'm not constrained by the rules of criminal procedure. If I want to shoot off your balls with the thirty-eight I have aimed at them, there won't be any Internal Affairs investigation."

I pulled back the revolver's hammer. Fremont heard the click and looked down.

"How should I know where that psycho is?"

"You've got vans filled with true believers, armed with everything except pitchforks, looking for him."

He leaned forward. "If I knew where he was, why would I have to look for him?"

"Something went wrong at the courthouse."

The Clancy Brothers and Tommy Makem replaced Dennis Day on the jukebox.

"Albie Wilson didn't get himself killed to make a political statement," I said.

"Look, I already told the cops I don't know Wilson, and I don't know shit about what went down."

"That's not what his brother Noonan says."

Fremont leaned back in his chair. "I don't know no Noonan."

I fired the thirty-eight into the floor. Fremont yelped and bounced on his chair. There was another brief disturbance at the bar.

"I never could get into the game of chess," I said. "The idea of a stalemate disgusts me. There should be a winner and a loser."

"You're crazy, old man."

I fired again.

"Cut that shit out," Fremont screamed.

I leaned forward and stared into his eyes. "I hate to lose," I said.

Fremont was a small fish in a large pool, a piece of shit floating in an urban drainage pipe waiting to be flushed out. He oozed control and self-importance, and the half-wits who stood in his shadow worshipped him. From the time I was a kid on the Roxbury streets, I wanted only to bring down people like Dermott Fremont.

"The next time, I take out a kneecap."

"Albie Wilson acted on his own. It had nothing to do with Vigil. He got his brother to drive him. That's it."

"Van just pulled up, Doc," Waycross said. "Five males."

"Shoot them," I said.

Fremont's eyes flitted from the front window to Waycross and back to me. "You're bluffing," he said.

"Willy, where's my Guinness?" I called.

"Albie misjudged the security. That's the only way I can figure it. There wasn't supposed to be any hit, only fireworks. He must've panicked."

This time the disturbance behind me was louder and longer as Waycross disarmed Fremont's band of merry men and escorted them to a table.

Willy's hands shook as he placed my mug of Guinness on the table.

"'Tis a fine brew," I said. "So, what was the second car for?"

Fremont blanched. "What second car?"

He quickly held up his hands. "Don't fuckin' shoot," he said. "Insurance, okay? Albie wanted to know that he had a way out."

"Who drove the second car?"

"I swear I don't know."

I considered what he had told me. It was a start, but not much more than that. Another time, I thought, I would have a more private heart-to-heart with J-Cubed.

"Mr. Fremont, you and I are going to meet again," I said, pushing myself away from the table. "When that happens, it will be immaterial to me whether you answer my questions, or I blow off your fucking head. Have a pleasant evening."

WAYCROSS AND I WALKED TO MY RENTED Ford Explorer.

"Bolton used to say you needed a leash," he said. "I think a cage might be more appropriate."

"Fuck 'em if they can't take a joke," I said.

Waycross's laughter was muffled.

"You choking?" I asked him. "Need a whack on the back?"

"I'm fine," he said.

"I never thought to ask, Neville. What are you using for a weapon?"

"My service nine. I've kept it all these years."

We stepped into the parking lot, where Danny Kirkland leaned against my car. "Hey, Doc," he said. "I had to see if you'd come out of Riddle's alive."

"Sorry to disappoint you."

"You're reinventing the wheel. Have you asked yourself the next question yet? 'Why shoot up the courthouse?' If it ain't a hit, what the fuck is it?"

"What do you want?" I asked him.

"What I've been saying right along. I know stuff. You know other stuff. We compare. I save you some steps. You give me the whole story."

"Move," I said.

"Will you admit that there's more to this than Zrbny?"

"I'll get rid of him," Waycross said.

"No, Neville," I said, grabbing his arm. "Let's not compound our felony."

Kirkland stepped away from the car. "Good advice, Brother Waycross," he said.

Waycross and I slipped into the Explorer.

"Might be you gotta dig deeper, Doc," Kirkland said.

"Kind of you to point that out, Danny," I said.

"Might be you gotta go back fifteen years."

I slammed the door.

"Neville, I don't like cities," I said, guiding the vehicle through the snow. "I concur with my daughter Lane's assessment that I should not be allowed to roam freely through them. Anything might happen. This time it's your former boss's fault. I should be hibernating. I especially do not enjoy cases like this one."

"Where are we going?" he asked.

"I'm going to drop you off. I've got a date with a media mogul."

"I don't get to watch?" Waycross asked with a chuckle.

"Ha, now you've got the spirit," I said. "No."

He was silent, gazing at the snow.

"You enjoyed the confrontation back there," I said.

He hesitated. "I felt like I was doing something, getting somewhere."

"You didn't feel that in the Brotherhood?"

"Sometimes," he said. "Mostly it was like walking through a war zone and not being able to fire back at the snipers. Guess I never lost my cop's head."

"What did you do with the anger?" I asked.

"What do you mean?"

"You weren't drinking, you didn't return fire, and you stuck with the good-works mission."

"I seldom get angry," he said. "That's never been a problem."

I CLEARED SECURITY AND RODE THE EXpress elevator to twenty.

Wendy Pouldice had the only apartment on the floor. I stood outside her door with a bag full of the makings of dinner. She answered my knock immediately.

"I'll be damned," she said. "You made it through the blizzard."

"Crab curry?"

"And calisthenics?" she asked with a grin.

"We need to talk."

She shrugged, and the leer disappeared. "C'mon in, Lucas. I've already eaten."

I gave her the bag. "Freeze it. We'll do a rain check."

Braverman lay sprawled on a white sofa. He had graduated from *Bawdy Boston* to *People*.

"Later, Donald," Pouldice said.

The big man climbed from the sofa and let himself out.

"He doesn't say much," I observed.

"He's dependable," she said, lowering herself into a chair. "Sit."

I circled a low glass table and sat in a matching chair. "Felix Zrbny," I said.

"You're so single-minded, Lucas."

I shrugged. "Past behavior is still the best indicator of future behavior. Zrbny is dangerous."

In my years of practice, a patient's assertion of an intent to change was the least reliable forecaster that she would cease her drinking, or that he would stop abusing his wife and children. Psychological testing was a reasonable sample of a person's thoughts, attitudes, and feelings at the time of test administration. Characterological idiosyncrasies often emerged from an expertly administered and interpreted Thematic Apperception Test, a series of storytelling pictures developed by Henry Murray at Harvard in the 1930s. The trend in psychology, however, was away from projective testing and toward whatever could be measured. The field was counting its way to irrelevance.

Many times in court, I had been asked about the likelihood of a defendant's repeating the behavior that had brought him before the court. Occasionally I had a response; most often I admitted that I had no idea.

There was no doubt in my mind what the city would be dealing with if we did not get Zrbny off the streets.

All behavior has a context. Explosive violence has a complex choreography and usually an intrapsychic script. When the victims are strangers, they have walked onstage in act 2, or 3, or 5, without knowing their lines. Only the aggressor knows what is going on in his head and on his stage.

"You've talked with Zrbny," I said.

"Many times. He has a story to tell. There are questions that he wants to answer."

"He's a fugitive. He can't pop in off the streets to titillate your viewers."

She shrugged. "We'll see."

"Wendy, he's already killed today. I don't know what trips his wire, but when he goes, more people will die."

"I think you're wrong," she said. "People do change."

"Sure. He's killing at a slower pace."

Legs in her white linen suit crossed, hands planted firmly on the chair arms, Wendy Pouldice knew something that no one else knew. I suspected that it was not enough to keep her from getting killed.

"You've seen him since he escaped," I said.

She continued to smile. "Lucas, we've been friends for a long time."

"Forget the rest of the speech," I said, and shoved myself from the back-killing chair.

I unfolded the copy of the Escher print that I had found in Zrbny's desk and dropped it on the glass table. "Recognize anyone?"

She leaned forward and stared at the black-and-white forms plodding their way through stone emptiness—oblivious and alone. Pouldice grabbed the print and focused on the face at its center, the faded publicity shot.

"I had a midday show and anchored the evening news back then," she said. "Where did you get this?"

"Fifteen years ago your crew was the first at Ravenwood."

"Lucas, answer my question."

"Zrbny called you that day, didn't he?"

She dropped the print on the table, slammed her hands to her hips, and stared at the ceiling.

"Wendy, you're going to get yourself killed, and you're exposing others to that risk."

"We're all going to die, Lucas. I don't plan on doing it soon."

"When do you expect him?"

As if on cue, Braverman strode into the room and stood at the door.

"That guy is amazing," I said.

I retrieved the Escher print.

"If we can't talk about Zrbny, what about Dermott Fremont?"

She glanced quickly at Braverman. "Vigil," she said. "We've been reporting the courthouse story since this morning."

"Fremont?"

"What about him? I don't know the man. My people have tried to interview him. He refuses."

I looked at Braverman. "Donald, what sort of guy is J-Cubed?"

The big guy's answer was to pull open the door and hold it for my exit.

"You've got him well trained," I told her.

"The business has changed, Lucas. We don't just report the game. We're players now."

Wendy Pouldice was setting herself up as an accessory to whatever horror Felix Zrbny visited on the city. "You're not at the zoo," I said. "You're not watching animals behind an electric fence and across a moat."

She said nothing.

Braverman cleared his throat and I left.

ON THE TWENTY-MINUTE DRIVE FROM THE Towers to Bolton's office, I began to have a feel for what churned at the back of my mind. Vigil was not making a political statement with its assault on the courthouse. Albie Wilson, however crazy he was, had his half-brother driving the only car that concerned Wilson. The second car and driver were for a different passenger, one who had not arrived in court. I was convinced that Vigil wanted Zrbny free and alive. What I did not know was why.

Bolton met me at his door. "The little guy in there is Benjamin Moffat," he said. "He just survived a face-off with Zrbny."

"Is he reliable?"

"He's a ward attendant at the criminal psych unit. Worked with Zrbny for five years. He was on his way home from his shift at the hospital, saw Zrbny and pulled over."

"Where?" I asked.

"The Riverway, off Huntington."

"I was just out there," I said, thinking that Pouldice and Zrbny now shared the same cage.

"Zrbny aimed a gun at him and told him to go home. Moffat says there was a witness, a young woman standing in an apartment doorway. I've got units at both ends of the drive, and two unmarked cars moving onto the street."

I followed Bolton to his car and climbed in. "Why didn't he shoot Moffatt?" I asked.

"You're supposed to tell me that."

Bolton made the turn onto a deserted Huntington Avenue. "I have a tactical unit on standby," he said. "We're treating this as a hostage situation."

"Is Zrbny holding the woman?"

"Moffatt doesn't know. Zrbny was on the street. The woman was in the doorway. He said it looked like she lives there. Moffatt didn't know the street number, but he described the area well. He was happy not to be shot. He drove off. Zrbny just stood in the road."

It made sense that Zrbny would hole up somewhere. He was a killer on the run in a crippling snowstorm.

. . . residents attempting to purchase hand-guns, and when they realize they can't, buying large hunting knives, crowding hardware stores for lengths of pipe, and garden centers for everything from hedge clippers to chainsaws. Community humane societies like this one in suburban Needham report hundreds of applications from people seeking to adopt dogs, the bigger and more vicious, the better. The city is in a panic. There can be no question about that. We're in for a long night. . . .

CHAPTER 16

SABLE SAT IN THE DARKENED APARTMENT.

The aquarium's rainbow colors had washed to a mud gray. The gentle noise of bubbling water was gone.

"The electricity went off," Sable said. "I didn't think you were coming back."

I stood at the door and watched the road. Someone had followed me from the Towers. I noticed him when I crossed the bridge. When I stopped at the corner, he froze in the shadows a hundred yards away. I did not see him now.

A car moved slowly past and parked. The engine idled, and no one got out of the car.

"Mr. Guzman sent flowers," I said, dropping the bag on the sofa beside her.

I retrieved the shotgun from the bathroom and returned to the front window.

"Felix, what's going on?" Sable asked.

"He said you should put them in water."

A TV satellite truck stopped on the other side of the river.

"Go into the kitchen," I said. "Now."

I heard her leave the room.

A van turned onto the Riverway and came fast, sliding to a halt thirty yards away. Four men climbed out, talked briefly, then dispersed toward the buildings. The TV truck's klieg lights snapped on and illuminated the street and the blowing snow.

I moved back through the apartment to the cellar door.

"Felix?"

"Stay away from the front," I said, and stepped into the cellar.

I followed emergency lighting through the subterranean corridor. In each building's cellar, metal barrels overflowed with cans, milk cartons, bottles, tins. Some tenants had not bothered with the barrels and dropped their debris on the floor.

I had not gone far when I heard noise behind me. Someone opened Sable's door. I waited until the door slammed shut.

Ducking pipes and wires, I ran the length of the hall until I reached the last cellar. That's when I heard gunshots.

I climbed stairs to the first-floor entry. Three teenagers stood outside the door watching the action on the street. More shots were fired.

When I pushed open the street door, one kid looked at me, then at the shotgun. "They after you, mister?"

I nodded.

His friends turned. "That's Vigil," a second one said. "You don't want to fuck with them. They got a shootout going with the cops."

The third kid, a tall, gangly adolescent, spoke up. "If you don't shoot me with that, I'll show you another way out of here."

I nodded.

"C'mon."

I followed him into the building and down the stairs. He crossed the hall, dodged garbage mounds, and slipped behind the furnace to the wall.

"You reach up there," the kid said, "you'll feel loose boards. Slide 'em to the right, then haul yourself out. There's a fence with a hole ripped in it. Go through there, between the two buildings, and you'll come out on the next block."

He moved aside, and a voice shouted, "Freeze."

The kid backed across the cellar.

"I don't want you. I want the big guy."

The kid turned to run. Automatic weapon fire cut him down.

I waited until the shooter stepped cautiously into sight beyond the furnace, then fired two rounds from the Mossberg. He caromed off the wall on his way down.

More men approached, running through the corridor. When they were only yards away, I stepped from behind the furnace and fired.

I SAT IN THE CAR WITH BOLTON WATCHING tactical officers escort handcuffed vigilantes to a van, and listening to muffled bursts of gunfire from somewhere inside the building. Our back seat was the temporary repository for seized weapons, mostly Mac-10s and Uzis. At random intervals, the door opened and a cop contributed to the arsenal.

There was one knife in the pile of metal—a bone-handle with a twelve-inch blade that was at least two inches across and sharpened on both edges. "Asshole was hunting bears on the Riverway," I muttered.

Bolton glanced through the snow at the TV lights on the far side of the river. "How did BTT get here so fast?" he asked.

I followed his gaze. "It's their neighborhood."

"That truck was parked there when my units came on the scene. Then Vigil came sliding in and turned the street into a battle zone."

"Scanners?"

"We used a scrambled channel."

I shrugged. "Any sign of Zrbny?"

"Nothing yet."

A tac officer tapped on Bolton's window. "We found a woman inside. She's incoherent, hiding under a table in the kitchen. She doesn't appear to be injured."

We followed the cop through the basement apartment. A female officer leaned against the sink. She aimed her flashlight at a row of pill bottles on a shelf, Thorazine and Mellaril among others, prescribed for Sable Bannon.

I looked under the table where the young woman lay in the shadows, curled in fetal position and facing the wall. Her meds were antipsychotics. I had no way to know what reality she had created for herself when Zrbny passed through followed by Vigil and a cadre of heavily armed police officers, and gunfire exploded in and around her home.

My own experience, and the work of pioneering Scottish analyst R. D. Laing, had taught me that I had to enter her world. With gunfire echoing in the cellar, I had to work fast. My first step was to lower myself to the floor and sit, to be physically on the same plane with her.

"Ms. Bannon, my name is Lucas."

I expected no response, and I received none. It was time to acknowledge the obvious.

"You've had a difficult day. When you are ready, you can tell me about it. I'd like to hear your voice, to hear what you have to say."

The embedded instructions defined our roles: she will be able and willing to talk; I will listen.

I waited a moment, then verbally tugged at the frightened woman. "I didn't think my knees were going to allow me to sit down here. They don't always cooperate. This time they did."

"I forgot to feed my fish," she said.

"I'd like to help you do that now. You'll have to show me where you keep the food, and how much you feed them."

"That's when I take my pills."

It was a paired association, something that I had often seen among my patients.

"I noticed the medications on the shelf. Would you like to do that now?"

"Fish first," she said, peering over her shoulder at me.

I extended my hand and she grabbed it, holding tight as she twisted around and slowly emerged from beneath the table. A burst of radio chatter from the hall startled her.

"That's a police radio," I said.

"Okay."

She continued to move forward, held my forearm with her other hand, and we helped each other stand.

Bolton stepped into the doorway and said, "Lucas, get her out of here now."

Sable Bannon tried to pull away, to retreat to her secure world under the table. I grabbed her around the waist.

A cop yelled from the cellar. "They're coming out. Clear the fucking area."

Another voice screamed, "Officer down."

I half carried the trembling woman through the hall to the front of her apartment. Radio chatter was constant. Gunfire in the cellar was close.

"We'll be safe outside," I said.

She struggled less as we approached the front door. "Okay," she whispered. "Wait. My flowers."

She grabbed a paper bag from the sofa and held it to her throat.

Cops inside and outside cleared the doorway for us. One wrapped a blanket over her shoulders. We stepped from the warm apartment illuminated only by the streaks and arcs of flashlights, into a whipping, frigid blizzard illuminated by blinding banks of TV lights across the Muddy River. I shielded my eyes and tried to locate Bolton's cruiser in the sea of vehicles and humanity that clogged the Riverway.

The man who emerged from the crowd smiled. I hesitated because I thought he wanted to tell me something. Then I saw the small-caliber handgun, heard three sharp cracks, and felt Sable Bannon go limp and slip from my arms.

I remember thinking that this was where a movie shifted to slow motion and the sound distorted, or black and white replaced color.

The flowers that spilled from her bag were yellow. The blood that bubbled from her mouth and spilled onto the snow was red. The crowd noise—the panicked screams, the shouted directions—played at the correct speed.

I dove into the crowd and tackled the smiling man. The gun fell from his hand and disappeared in the snow. There was nothing slow about my repeated hammering of his face.

I wanted the smile to disappear.

I wanted him dead.

. . . don't know how many are dead. We've heard three. We've heard as many as nine. What we know for certain is that Felix Zrbny was inside the building when the confrontation with tactical officers began. We don't know if Zrbny is among the dead. Bob, I don't recall a day like this. The assault on the courthouse where three died, the accident that resulted in Zrbny's escape, now this. I talked with one witness who described the scene in the building's cellar. He said there were bodies all over the place. We will continue our nonstop coverage. I understand that we are now providing national and international feeds, and don't forget that there are summaries of the day's events, and background information at our web site, WWW dot . . .

CHAPTER 18

EDDIE HAD QUIT SHOVELING FOR THE NIGHT. The snow was deep on the Towers' esplanade.

I avoided the main entrance and followed the ramp that led to the underground parking area. I waited only a few minutes until the steel garage doored cranked open and a car drove out. I slipped from the shadows and ducked inside.

At the rear, beyond the rows of cars, a security guard sat in an enclosed area behind a desk, watching silent monitors, video shots of hallways and elevators. As I approached, I saw that one of the monitors was a muted version of Bob Britton at the BTT news desk. His mouth moved. His face twisted in mock astonishment.

I pulled open the glass door and stepped inside.

A shot of the Riverway row-apartment buildings replaced Britton on the monitor. A banner at the bottom of the screen read *Viewer Discretion Advised*.

The security guard turned in his chair. "Can I help you?" he asked.

I stared at the TV as the camera closed in on a man with his arm around Sable. She had a blanket thrown across her shoulders, and the man protected her from the crowd, the storm, and the lights.

"They've been showing that for the last half hour," the guard said. "Gruesome. You got some ID?"

"Wendy Pouldice is expecting me."

"She give you a card?"

I fished in my pockets, then froze. The monitor showed a man shove his way through the crowd. Sable spun away from her protector and fell. The old man who had been guiding her surged after the shooter and dragged him to the snow-covered street. Then Britton's silent running mouth returned to the screen.

"What happened to her?" I asked.

"The girl? She's dead."

The pain at the back of my neck shot into my spine. As I turned and walked slowly away from the desk, the buzzing in my head threatened to topple me.

"Mister, you okay?"

I continued to walk.

My eyes watered, my vision blurred.

Insects buzzed on a distant summer day. There was no snow, and everyone except me expected my sister Levana to walk through the door at any minute.

"Hey. You can't get out that way."

The guard approached from behind. "How did you get in here, anyway?" he asked.

I stopped walking and pressed my hands against the sides of my head. He continued to talk. I heard noise, but the only words I understood were those whispered inside my head: "The dead never do come back to life."

I turned, grabbed him by the throat, and lifted him from the pavement. He squirmed, kicked, emitted gurgling noises, drooled, and eventually died.

I STEPPED FROM THE ELEVATOR ON THE SECond floor and walked to the studio doors. When I opened the door, a young woman with a clipboard leaned against me to push me back into the hall. I grabbed her and threw her. She landed with a crack halfway to the elevator, her clipboard clattering against the wall and across the floor.

I entered the set and closed the door. The person operating the camera held up four fingers, then three, two, and pointed at Bob Britton, who looked up from a sheaf of papers with dramatic flair.

"For those of you just joining us," the anchor said, in a throaty baritone that sounded nothing like the voice I had heard in Guzman's, "we're going to return live to the scene of the 'Riverway Shootout,' but first we're going to replay the tape of an incident from earlier this evening. What you're about to see is real. It happened less than an hour ago. We advise viewer discretion due to the explicit violence that is certain to upset some viewers."

Britton returned to his pile of papers.

The camera operator waited while the tape ran. After a moment he said, "Bob," and began his finger countdown.

"At the center of today's eruption of violence in the city," Britton began, "is one man, mass murderer Felix Zrbny."

I moved through the darkened studio to Britton's left.

"On an August day fifteen years ago," he continued, "the teenaged Zrbny embarked on a rampage that became known as the 'Ravenwood Massacre.' Zrbny stalked, savagely attacked, and killed three times that day. His choice of weapon was his father's butcher knife, honed razor-sharp for cutting meat. His first victim was thirty-one-year-old Shannon Waycross, the wife of former Boston homicide detective Neville Waycross. She was the last victim found, her body discovered by her husband after he had disarmed and arrested Zrbny in front of the home of victim number three, Florence Dayle. The teenager fled to the Dayle residence after killing eighteen-year-old Gina Radshaw, a Ravenwood High School graduate who planned to attend Dartmouth College and pursue a career in business. Sources familiar with the investigation denied that any of the victims had been sexually assaulted. An expert on sexual homicide, investigative psychologist Fawn Hocksley-Bernquist, joins us now from our Providence studio. She is the author of the widely acclaimed Serial

Murder, Sexual Motive. *Welcome to 'Boston Tonight,' and to our continuing coverage of the 'Riverway Shootout,' Dr. Hocksley-Bernquist."*

As he listened to his expert's response, I stepped into the light and onto the set.

CHAPTER 19

"NONE OF THIS NEEDED TO HAPPEN," I said, rubbing my sore hands.

Bolton sat beside me in the cruiser's back seat. "I hope you're not blaming yourself, Lucas."

I shook my head. "No one person could create a mess like this."

"You break any bones?"

"My hands hurt like hell. Nothing's broken."

Bolton's people had wanted to do their job quietly. Seize Zrbny, lock him up, and go from there. Instead, Dermott Fremont's crazy militia group and a media unconstrained by its own ethics had created a carnival of violence. By morning, politicians everywhere would be yelling about gun control, shoving God back into our lives, assigning armed guards at arcades and movie theaters, bringing unrestrained immorality and violence under control—as if there were a causal link between the two and anyone gave a shit.

"We don't get to take a commercial break, do we?"

"No brew at halftime," Bolton said.

"Any sign of Zrbny?"

"We found where he climbed out of the cellar. He emptied the shotgun at Vigil, drove them back at us, then ran. Tactical tracked him a block east. A snowplow wiped out his tracks."

"Who killed Sable Bannon?"

"We haven't identified him yet. He has the tattoo."

I watched snow swirl past the car. "Why?"

There was no answer to that question—not yet, maybe not ever. Bolton was silent, staring at the palms of his hands as if he might discover an answer there.

I came to Boston to observe a man, and to offer my impressions to an assistant attorney general. May Langston was dead. So was the judge.

And I was caught in the middle of a war.

"What's tonight's body count?" I asked.

"Three Vigil dead, one wounded. One seventeen-year-old kid dead. Two officers wounded. Sable Bannon, age twenty-five, dead."

He recited the dismal numbers. He knew them, would adjust them if they changed, and he would not forget.

"One of the tactical officers is in critical condition," he added.

"This case is haunted," I said. "It's been haunted since 1984."

"What are you thinking?"

I gazed beyond the klieg lights to the Towers, barely visible through the snow. "Neville Waycross radioed for backup in Ravenwood. Wendy Pouldice arrived. That day made her."

"That day, some earlier help from Levana Zrbny's disappearance, and the Stallings case."

"What did she have to do with those two?"

"She had the inside track on both of them."

"Educate me," I said.

"I told you she lived in Ravenwood then. She took on Levana Zrbny's disappearance as a personal crusade. Missing Persons had the case listed as unexplained. Pouldice called it an abduction, campaigned against the PD's classification system, faulted us for inadequate response, and claimed to have a source who witnessed a man in a white car grab the kid."

I wondered just how far back Pouldice and Felix Zrbny went. "What about Stallings?" I asked.

"That was a witnessed abduction."

"I remember. The kid who saw it go down was so traumatized that she couldn't tell you much."

"Under hypnosis she remembered the white car parked near the playground a few days before the abduction, and the man with red hair."

"How did she describe what she saw that day?"

"You can look at the file if you want. Several times she got to the point where she could say, 'He took Theresa away,' but that was it. She'd become hysterical then. We don't know if the redhead took

Theresa. We don't know if the white car was involved."

"What was Pouldice's angle on it?"

"Another crusade. She donated the first five thousand dollars to the Stallings Fund, bought her way into the family. She did weekly stories for a year, generated a few leads, but nothing that went anywhere. She still does occasional features on the story. She called me a couple of months ago about the case."

"What did she want?"

"She made an appointment to come in, then never showed."

From the time I slid into Logan Airport, I felt as if I were riding a roller coaster operated by a drunk. I wanted to allow my mind to float on a sea of possibilities but I had no time. I was playing a game of catch-up and I hated it.

Albie Wilson could not have anticipated the change in security arrangements at the court-house. He also had no way of knowing that Felix Zrbny was not in the courtroom. I believed that Wilson was there to liberate Zrbny.

Why would they want him out?

Bolton said that BTT arrived at the Riverway first, followed by Vigil. Neither outfit could have monitored the radio traffic. When I asked Wendy Pouldice about J-Cubed, she shot a look at her hired help. Perhaps I had stumbled into an unholy alliance between BTT and Vigil.

"Where's Neville?" I asked.

"When you dropped him at the office, he went back to reading case files. Something in one of the reports hammered Neville hard. He nearly flew out of there. I'm afraid he'll climb into a bottle, do some serious damage to himself. He's already had a stroke. I've got a couple of people looking for him."

"What did he see in the file?"

Bolton shook his head. "I figure it had something to do with Shannon's murder."

"I'm going back to the Towers," I said. "I think there's a connection between BTT and Vigil. I also think that Pouldice has talked to Zrbny since this morning."

"Why would she tell you anything now?"

"Maybe if I neuter her battery-operated Neanderthal, she'll be more receptive to my naturally charming self."

"I'm told that Braverman often quotes lengthy passages from *Bawdy Boston*."

I opened the car door. "Like I said. He's a fucking Neanderthal."

"How do you propose to neuter a guy that size?"

"Swiss Army knife," I said, slamming the door and weaving my way through the haphazardly parked vehicles, the mob scene, and the drifting snow.

I had no idea what I would do. I knew only that I had to do something.

· · ·

THE SECURITY OFFICER WAS NOT AT HIS post. Probably making rounds, I thought. I grabbed the desk phone to call Pouldice's apartment. The line was dead.

"What a fucking outfit," I muttered.

The elevator allowed me to enter, but refused to accept the third floor as a destination. The offices were closed. I punched 20, and a virtual voice instructed me to enter my identification number.

"I'm not trying to make a fucking withdrawal," I growled.

I hit 2, which the machinery accepted. I felt the thrust upward, listened to the muted whirring, and waited until the computer-controlled box settled into a landing at what it considered the second floor. The doors opened and I stepped into the corridor.

The studio's red On Air light was illuminated. The building had security personnel, so it must have a security office, I reasoned.

I walked back to the elevator and reviewed the directory. The lobby was one choice, but no one had been there, so I went with number two, the parking garage.

This time the doors opened on a glass-enclosed space containing a desk, a bank of security monitors, and no guard. "Where are the cops when you need them?" I muttered.

I fished in my pockets until I found my reading

glasses, then examined a telephone two feet wide, with more buttons than a Hammond organ. It would not be long until an engineering degree was required to call next door.

A typed list to the right of the handset included "Ms. Pouldice—9#20." I was making progress.

I grabbed the phone, punched the requisite keys, and looked up as I listened to the ring. One of the monitors was a silent feed from BTT. The camera focused on a guy with a bad hairpiece who, I assumed, was thinking he looked dignified and sounded knowledgeable. I have always considered tabloid TV more insidious than the printed crap that greets me at the supermarket checkout. Someone with an oiled voice—Stone Phillips, say—will always be more influential and incite more fantasies than a printed headline next to the Tic-Tacs and Bic lighters.

The phone continued to ring. When no one answered after a dozen rings, I hung up.

The man identified at the bottom of the screen as Bob Britton continued to flap his soundless mouth. I watched, expecting his toupee to topple onto the desk. Instead, the screen divided. The woman on the right was Dr. Fawn Hyphenated, Providence, R. I., author of, expert on.

"Aren't we all," I said.

I turned, thinking that I would walk back to the Riverway, but when I saw the monitor's reflection in the glass, I looked at the screen. I seldom watch

TV, but I know that talking heads do not jog around the set.

On the left, Britton was on his feet attempting to struggle with a much larger man. On the right, Dr. Fawn continued to pontificate.

I ran for the elevator.

. . . lost contact with Bob Britton in our studio. We will stay with you live from our Riverway location. We have only preliminary information on events inside the buildings. Mass murderer Felix Zrbny was holding a young woman hostage in the apartment you see on your screen. You can also see the heavy police presence at the entrance. When tactical officers stormed the building, Zrbny fled into the cellar. A shootout ensued, with what we would describe as heavy automatic weapons fire. We've counted two body bags thus far. We don't know if Zrbny is among the dead. We're simply not getting cooperation from . . .

CHAPTER 20

I SHOVED OPEN THE STUDIO DOOR AND waited until my eyes adjusted to the light. Pain stung my neck and upper spine. I felt as if colonies of insects crept and buzzed inside my head.

A gray-haired, bearded man crouched beside the woman I had thrown into the hall. I removed the handgun from my pocket and walked slowly forward, studying the man's profile. When I was ten feet away, he looked up. I raised the gun, and aimed at his face.

His eyes were empty. Like mine, I thought. Dead eyes.

Then I recognized him. He was the old man who had tried to protect Sable. I felt no fear in him. I had no desire to kill him, but I did not know why. He said nothing. He continued to look at me, but he remained silent.

I walked to the elevator, punched the button and waited.

The old man returned his attention to the woman.

CHAPTER 21

WHEN I LOOKED INTO FELIX ZRBNY'S EYES, I knew I had nothing to fear from him. I did not know why.

He had hurled the young TV producer like a rag doll, breaking her arm and collarbone. He held a nine-millimeter handgun aimed at my face.

I am not a fan of death, especially my own. Whether I am to be in or out of the coffin, I do not like the notion of funerals. Zrbny's eyes held no life, but neither did they hold my death. He moved past me to the elevator, punched the Down button, and, after an endless span of time, stepped into the metal box and disappeared.

I opened the door to the studio, grabbed a wall phone immediately to my right, and dialed 911. When I made clear who and where I was, the nature of the emergency, and where Bolton was, the dispatcher told me to stay on the line. I told her I could not do that, left the phone off the hook, and moved into the set.

A camera technician lay unconscious against the wall. His breathing was good, his pulse strong.

Dr. Fawn's mouth continued to flap on a silent monitor. Behind the news desk, Britton, his head twisted at an impossible angle to his body, had become BTT's latest news flash. Felix Zrbny had broken his neck.

TWENTY MINUTES LATER, BOLTON AND I stood in the hall outside the studio watching medical technicians prepare the young woman for transport. "We found a dead security guard in the parking garage," he said. "Looks like Zrbny started there."

"Everyone's dispensable when it comes to the evening news," I said. "Even the news anchor."

"You think Vigil wanted Zrbny free?" Ray Bolton asked. "What for?"

"Story value," I said. "BTT is international hot shit right now."

"Tell me how it works."

"I'm not sure of any of this, Ray. Let's say Pouldice got to know Zrbny when his sister disappeared. When he was ready to pillage Ravenwood two years later, Zrbny called Pouldice."

I gave Bolton the copy of Escher's "Relativity" with Pouldice's old publicity photo. "I found that in Zrbny's bedroom. In the print the figures move around on different planes, oblivious to one another. They don't see. They don't touch. Pouldice sees everything. When I talked with her earlier, she tried to tell me that Zrbny had changed. Why would she bother?"

"She has an investment in him," Bolton said.

"I can't prove any of it."

"Lucas, you said that Zrbny was probably going to walk from that hearing. I agree. Why couldn't he wait a couple of days for Devaine to unlock the door for him?"

"Maybe he didn't know what was going down."

"Then how were they going to get him out of there?"

"Driver number two. Fremont confirmed that there was a second car. He says Albie Wilson wanted insurance."

Bolton considered my theory. "It could be that simple. Why would Zrbny camp on the Riverway? What was he doing here? Why kill Britton?"

"They fucked with him. Don't ask me how. Where was his lawyer this morning? Who the fuck is his lawyer?"

Bolton sighed. "Hensley Carroll out of Jamaica Plain."

"What's his claim to fame?"

"He's defended members of Vigil. Carroll isn't connected to the group. He's been around the system for years."

"Has he done any work for BTT?"

"I don't know. I'd say that's out of his league."

"Where was he this morning? What was his excuse?"

"He didn't call the court. Lucas, don't mess with Carroll. He's Zrbny's attorney."

Bolton's last remark was a caution. Hensley Carroll lived life behind a shield of confidentiality and privilege.

"Maybe you can't talk to him," I said. "Anyone find Waycross?"

"They're still looking. Lucas . . ."

This time Bolton's tone was more than cautionary.

"I'll be nice," I said.

I FOUND THE LAWYER'S JAMAICA PLAIN address. His office was downstairs, his home upstairs. He was still awake.

"I've been sitting here watching this shit on the tube," Hensley Carroll said. "Yeah, I saw you on there too. Listen, Boston's got its problems but mostly it's a quiet town. I don't remember anything like this. You want coffee?"

"Sounds good."

"I'll make a fresh pot. Since my wife passed, rest her soul, I have trouble sleeping."

The short, bald, heavyset Carroll busied himself in the kitchen. I watched BTT report the latest carnage from outside their headquarters. They could not get in; Bolton had sealed the building as a crime scene.

"It's fuckin' wild when you think about it," Carroll said as he returned and settled his bulk into his recliner. "Back in the sixties when the strangler was on the loose, you had to wait for the last evening paper to find out if anybody got whacked. Now they've got this shit on TV while it's happening. Amazing. Well, shit. We put guys on the moon, I guess. Coffee'll be about ten minutes. Sit down, Doc. Friends call me Hink."

I wondered what his enemies called him. "You are Felix Zrbny's attorney."

He tapped a Camel from his pack and put a match to it. "That's a lot of why I'm glued to this TV set. I figured with all the media the case would be good for business, you know? I don't know why it matters. I don't need the business. Never got to meet Zrbny."

Carroll took a long drag on his cigarette. "I don't know how many times I've been before David Devaine, rest his soul. I told that shithead a dozen times if I told him once. When it's snowin', I don't go out that fuckin' door. Busted my hip fifteen years ago walking through sleet on South Huntington. I don't do snow. When they shovel and spread salt, then I go out."

"You didn't call the court."

Both eyebrows shot up. "Why the fuck should I? Because his honor's got a bee up his ass? Hah."

"Did Zrbny retain you, Hink?"

"Look, Doc, this is my town, too, okay? I don't want that sick fuck running around loose. That's why I'm talking to you. I don't have to tell you shit and you know it."

He crushed his cigarette into a green ceramic ashtray. "Two months ago this big fucker came into my office downstairs. No appointment, no nothing. Doesn't have a fuckin' name, I figure, because he doesn't introduce himself. He pushes an envelope across my desk. Will I represent Felix Zrbny through the hearing process? There's no prep involved, he says. Burden's on the Commonwealth. All I gotta do is show up. There's a fuckin' bank check for twenty grand in the envelope. I about creamed my gabardine. No way I'm gonna say no to that. The next morning I'm reading about me in the newspapers."

"What about case files, meeting your client?"

"The guy specifically said I was not to go to the hospital and talk to Zrbny. I asked about court records. He said if I wanted to read that shit, it was up to me, but I didn't have to waste my time. The guy was dirty. I knew that. I also knew there wasn't anything wrong with me taking that check. Zrbny's case wasn't dope or kiddie porn."

He shrugged. "I deposited the fuckin' check."

"That's it?"

"Coffee's ready. Wait a sec."

Carroll shoved himself from his chair and disappeared into the kitchen. He was back in minutes with two mugs of coffee that tasted as good as it smelled.

"Doc, I was born in this house," he said, lowering himself into his chair and firing up another Camel. "I spent two years in the army, one in Korea. The rest of the time I've been right here. I know this city. I may be greedy, but I ain't a fuckin' fool. I had a buddy downtown run the plate on the big guy's car. It came back to that outfit right there."

He pointed at his Magnavox TV. "Boston Trial Television. That's all I needed to know. I figured if anything kicked back on me, I knew where to find him."

. . . is dead. Boston Trial Television news anchor Bob Britton was doing what he has been doing so well for so many years, broadcasting the news. Mass murderer Felix Zrbny invaded the BTT studios, severely injuring producer Meg Waterman and engineer Ted Hanley, and killing Britton. We are stunned, shocked. The Towers, home of Pouldice Media, is a crime scene. Police are allowing no one to enter the building because Felix Zrbny may still be in there. We will continue from here, recognizing our obligation to viewers to provide uninterrupted . . .

CHAPTER 22

I WAITED UNTIL NO CARS WERE IN SIGHT,
then jumped and grabbed the maple tree branch,
hands slipping, but hauling myself into the tree. In
seconds a car passed; by then I was invisible.

The snow was heavier, the wind stronger. The
cold invaded my bones and stiffened my joints. My
fingers were numb. I had little time to rest. I needed
warmth and safety, and I knew where I would find
both.

My fingers slipped through the snow coating the
limb above my head. I grasped it and maneuvered
myself to the end of the branch. My foot slipped, but
I held on, and cleared the wall and its rack of razor
wire. Then I waited again.

The yard below was dark. I could barely see the
cars in the lighted parking lot fifty yards south.
Hearing nothing but the wind, I released my grip
and dropped into two feet of snow.

A light flashed across the yard, sweeping slowly
from a row of wintering lilac bushes toward me. I
dropped into the snow on my back, staring up at the

approaching light. The beam never slowed, passed me, then died.

As quickly as I could, pumping my legs in and out of the deep drifts, I moved across the yard to the rear of the building. I counted basement windows until I arrived at number seven.

The steel grid yielded to my grip as I knew it would. I rapped my knuckles against the glass.

There was no light, no sound within. I tapped a second time, and a dim light appeared through the smoky glass.

There was a shuffling noise, then, barely above a whisper, "That you, Felix?"

"Open up, Ralph," I said.

He flipped the window bar and turned the crank.

I crawled through the opening headfirst. The concrete floor was six feet below, but Ralph grabbed my belt and guided me slowly down. I lay still on my back, feeling the heat from the steam furnace in the adjacent room.

"Felix, oh Jesus, are you okay? I was sleeping. I watched about you on TV until midnight. I couldn't keep my eyes open after that."

He tugged my arm. "Tell me you're okay, Felix."

"I'm tired and cold, Ralph. That's all. I'm fine."

"I knew you'd come back. I just knew it. I got a place for you. Nobody will ever find you. I saved you some food. That's how sure I was."

Ralph Amsden had been in the hospital for thirty-five of his sixty years. He was a toothpick of a man with white hair, bulging eyes, and one arm. When new patients met Ralph, they figured that the hospital kept him because he knew the ancient furnace and all its quirks. He did not look crazy, and only occasionally talked crazy. A few people asked why he was hospitalized at all.

Ralph was born in Boston, grew up in Jamaica Plain, entered the army at eighteen, married at twenty-two. On the day after his twenty-fifth birthday, he killed his wife, her parents, her two brothers, then took the subway to Fenway Park, watched five innings of the Orioles humbling the Red Sox, and killed a hot dog vendor.

Ralph Amsden would never leave the hospital, and that was fine with him. His only visitor had been a sister, Terry. Twice a year she made the trip by subway and bus from Jamaica Plain. She brought photographs of her kids; Ralph did not know them, and would never meet them. Terry died in 1996, and whatever real contact Ralph had with the outside world died with her.

Years earlier he had modified the basement window. It appeared secure, but in seconds became a route to freedom. Ralph figured he might have a use for it someday, but not for himself.

"You gotta fix my window," he said now. "If anybody walks by, they'll see it."

I considered reminding him of the storm, telling him that no one would be out for a stroll behind the hospital through two feet of snow. Ralph would not be reassured. I pushed myself from the floor, reached out and grabbed the steel grate, and yanked it into place.

"The snow will cover my tracks," I said.

"You can't be coming and going, Felix. Jesus. They'll find you for sure."

The next time I crawled through Ralph's window would be the last time, but I saw no need to tell him that. I cranked the window into place.

"I got something for you," I said, and reached into my jacket for the package of Twinkies and the candy bar that I had picked up on my way.

Ralph loved sweets. If the only foods on earth consisted of sugar, chocolate, and corn syrup, Ralph would be certain that he had arrived in heaven.

"Why'd they kill that girl?" he asked. "Jesus. They must've shown that twenty times. You gotta tell me the truth. I can't get true stuff from TV. They gotta sell me shit I don't want and couldn't buy even if I did want it. Why'd they shoot up the courtroom? You hungry?"

"I had some soup," I said, wondering how long it had been since I sat in Sable's kitchen with a bowl of chicken noodle and rice and a box of crackers.

Now she was dead.

When I turned and walked away from the security guard in the parking garage, my head flooded with noise, and pain arced from the back of my head into my spine. These were sensations that I knew well, electric surges that stimulated muscle, cartilage, and bone. My first experience with the arrhythmic pulsing ache had been that day, that hot summer, that year I knew I was less than complete without Levana.

Someone took her away from me.

"What courtroom are you talking about, Ralph?"

"The one you were going to until those assholes flipped the truck. If you got there when you were supposed to, you might be dead now. Well, you could've been dead a bunch of times today, I guess."

I sat on a folding chair and surveyed Ralph's domain, his home for the biggest part of his life. His bed was an army cot, in disarray now because he had been asleep when I rapped on the window. Usually the bed was made with military precision— sheets without a crease, blanket pulled tight to the pillows, then folded down. His bureau was a stack of cantaloupe crates containing his folded clothes and the few objects that were important to him. A crucifix hung on the wall above the bed; a Bible lay on the small table to one side. There was no other reading material in the room. Ralph's window on the world was his thirteen-inch black-and-white TV that Terry had brought him ten years earlier.

Steam pipes clanked overhead. The large space was filled with boxes of nonperishable hospital supplies—toilet paper, soap, shampoo, floor-cleaning solvent, paper towels. The lamp on the bedside table put out about forty watts of dusty yellow light. There was a single overhead light, but Ralph switched that on only during the day when he worked. When I asked him about the poor lighting, he told me that he did not need to see much, just enough to get by.

Ralph filled a pan with water from the tap at the mop sink and put it on his hot plate. "I'm gonna make us some instant," he said, and sat on his cot. "I knew some Wilsons growing up. That was in Jamaica Plain. I never heard of Albie Wilson, but he's from Chelsea. I don't think I ever knew anybody from Chelsea."

I did not interrupt him. Eventually, Ralph would tell me what I wanted to know.

"There wasn't any Vigil when I was outside," he said, pulling a cigarette from an open box on his table.

Watching Ralph light his cigarettes was an education in adaptability. He had lost his right arm in a laundry accident twenty years earlier. The Winston dangled from his mouth as he talked and manipulated a matchbook—flipped open the cover, liberated a match but did not detach it, closed the cover behind the match, folded the match with his thumb so that the head touched the strike plate, slid it to one side and released his thumb as the match ignited. It was a fluid motion, requiring only seconds until he was dragging on his smoke.

"This Albie Wilson was part of the Vigil gang, or whatever they call themselves," he continued. "He drove up in front of the courthouse, hopped out of the car with an automatic, ran up the steps scattering reporters like chickens when the fox jumps into the coop, and shot up the fucking place. Jesus. You weren't there because the fucking sheriffs don't know how to drive."

He laughed—a dry, crackling snicker—at his own humor. "Felix, why did you shoot that deputy?"

I thought about the bloody, semiconscious Finneran lying in the snow on Storrow Drive. "When I walked away from the crash," I told him, "it didn't feel right. There was something unfinished there. I didn't want anyone to have any misunderstanding about what I will do with freedom. I went back and shot him."

"I know what you mean," Ralph said, nodding. "A man's gotta finish what he starts."

He stood, and placed his cigarette in a row of burn marks on the table's edge. He poured hot water into two hospital mugs, dumped teaspoons of instant coffee into each mug, stirred them, then handed one to me, stuck his Winston in his mouth, and carried the second mug back to the bottom of his cot.

"What do you know about Vigil, Ralph?"

"When Terry used to visit, she told me about them. Bunch of fucking crazies want to set up their own government. Terry and her kids had an apartment near a bar called Riddle's. That's where these guys hang out. Well, they did back then. I don't know about now. Terry's boyfriend ran with that crowd. One night he didn't come home. She didn't mind so much 'cause the guy was an asshole. He used to beat her and the kids. They fished him out of the harbor a couple weeks later. One of the Vigil gang came by her place and gave her twenty bucks for groceries."

He tapped out his butt on the metal cot frame. "What do they want with you?"

I sipped my coffee. "That who came after me?"

Ralph laughed his short, harsh laugh. "Then you started shooting at them, right? And they came running the other way and the fucking cops mowed 'em down. They should be in here, and I should be out there . . . except I don't want to be out there."

"Who killed Sable?"

"That the girl? The guy who shot her is with Vigil, but they ain't said his name yet. She a friend?"

"She helped me," I said.

"Reminded me of when Jack Ruby shot Lee Harvey Oswald. I saw that on TV too. They were indoors and it wasn't snowing, but there came Ruby out of the crowd, just like that asshole tonight."

"Who was the old guy with her?"

"Jesus. He about beat that shithead to death. Bunch of cops had to pull him off. His name is Lucas Frank. Believe it or not, he's a fucking shrink. Not like the wimps we got around this place. Felix, did you really kill Bob Britton? All I saw was your back, then the picture went dead. I thought BTT was gonna tell your story, make you a celebrity, tell the fuckin' truth. Shit. I thought they was gonna let you finish what you started."

It was exactly what I had thought, until something did not feel right about the setup. Pouldice should not have expected me. She did not need her goon around, and I had told her that any talking must be just the two of us. She had someone like Britton working for her, a man filled with self-importance shoving his way among people without seeing them.

I pushed my hands through my long black hair. "I don't know what went wrong," I said.

"What are you gonna do now?"

"Get warm. Think. I'd like to get some sleep."

Ralph pointed to a plywood loft in the corner. "You see them cases of toilet paper? You push them aside, crawl in there, then shove 'em back across the front like you see them right now. There's a mattress up there, blankets, two pillows. You stay as long as you want."

I felt like an animal crawling into a cave. I lay on my back and stared at the pipes strapped with metal bands to the ceiling. Ralph switched off his lamp, and I gazed into blackness.

It was time to consider the adjustments that I needed to make, the corrections in space and time, and to those who move, unseeing, through those dimensions.

CHAPTER 23

SLEEP WAS ELUSIVE.

I rolled over at four A.M., glanced at the clock radio's digital display, then I faded. It seemed only moments later—slumber has a way of making hours feel like seconds—that I was deep in rapid-eye-movement sleep, the dream state.

My trip into the unconscious was a Cecil B. DeMille epic, complete with a cast of thousands—well, maybe dozens. I needed no technology to enhance the special effects, and there was nothing virtual about my reality.

I can sum up the dream in one sentence: I walked endlessly up and down stone stairways, through long castle halls, knowing there was no escape from what seemed to be a series of interlocking, multidimensional squares and rectangles. What my one sentence does not convey are the faces and shapes, my feelings of rage, and the notions of meeting people that I don't see, or seeing people that I can't meet.

I saw the slope of a slate roof at an odd angle—

too pitched—from the window where I stood. Fear of the height chilled me, but then I turned and there was no window, no roof, no possibility of a drop from an unreasonable height. A man sat in silence at a cabaret table sipping a glass of wine. When I walked to him, opened my mouth to speak, he might have been there, but I was gone, on another plane, watching a woman carry a basket on her head.

The experience was oddly enjoyable, and disconcerting. In sleep, I marveled at my dream's complexity. When I knew that I was dreaming, I could have opened my eyes, made the world simple again by focusing on the light beyond the window drapes or the glow from the clock radio. I did not want to stop. I wanted to prowl those halls, climb the stairs, test the air between me and other humans to see if I could penetrate it, touch him or her, engage in conversation, smile, *some* fucking thing.

If there can be another dimension to silence, I went there. It began to snow inside the castle walls, and no one cared—or no one noticed. There had been no sound, so there was nothing to be muted by the indoor blanket of white. All of us continued to trudge the halls.

Pounding broke the silence and cracked the snow shroud. I looked down, but the sound was up—from a window space with no glass. A dove distressed by the noise fluttered in and out. I searched for the source of the repeated, thunder-ous battering.

I had to open my eyes. The hammer-pounding was happening on my door.

"What the hell?" I mumbled, glancing at the clock. "Five-fucking-thirty."

I hauled myself out of bed and walked to the door. Through the peephole's fish-eye lens, I saw Bolton's distorted features. I opened the door.

"I can't sleep," he said, gliding past me into the room.

"You woke me up to tell me that?"

He tossed me a pack of Player's cigarettes. "I hate myself for that, but I figured it was the only way to get you to talk at this hour."

"Excellent bribe," I said, opening the box and lighting the cigarette that I had wanted hours ago.

"I figured if I was pissed off, you had to be. When you get that way, you smoke."

"So you wake me at five-thirty in the morning, when I've been asleep for an hour and a half. Which is more hazardous to my health?"

"Shut up and smoke."

I did, and enjoyed the quick nicotine rush, the satisfying feel of the cigarette between my fingers. "Okay, I'm awake," I said. "Now, not unhappily so. What do you want?"

"I don't understand what's going on here."

"Join the club."

"I think you should talk to Dr. Kelly."

"Zrbny's shrink? Why? I read his report."

"You've always said that reports aren't worth shit. 'Aseptic,' I think you called them. Kelly had the most recent contact with Zrbny. He's in D.C. I've got the number."

"You do it," I said, always aversive to phones. "I'll talk to him."

"It would be nice if you joined us here in the twenty-first century," he said, unfolding a piece of paper and punching numbers on the phone.

"Ray, this smoke is an excellent way to get me awake and keep me awake. No tobacco is good enough—"

"Got him," he said, handing me the phone.

"You woke him up?"

"He's on the line."

"You didn't offer him a smoke," I said, taking the phone. "Dr. Kelly? This is Lucas Frank."

We talked for thirty minutes. Kelly had kept up with Zrbny's exploits on TV, and online with his computer. Nothing had happened that surprised Kelly, he said, except the Vigil involvement.

"I know about Vigil," he said. "I've met J-Cubed. We were at a community resources meeting a couple of years ago. He said his concern was the neighborhoods. I think he's a white supremacist."

On the subject of Felix Zrbny, Kelly was equally emphatic. "I was going to testify about his lethality, his desire for recognition. I think I could have predicted this. I know I'm not supposed to say that."

No one in a mental health field can claim to know the future behavior of a subject. There are studies showing that a layperson's predictive ability is more accurate than a clinician's. The first outfit to land on Kelly would be the American Psychological Association. The psychiatric equivalent of that professional labor union had dropped on me a time or two, but I had beaten them off. Others were not so fortunate. Reprimands and citations flew like confetti at a field day. All of it was bullshit. If shrinks used their common sense nearly as much as they dove into the *Diagnostic and Statistical Manual* for guidance, their predictive record would be far less dismal.

I asked Kelly, "Can you think of any reason why Vigil would want Zrbny free?"

"Felix wants celebrity. Boston Trial Television can give him that. The woman who runs that outfit—I think her name is Pouldice—is somehow connected with J-Cubed. I don't know the whole story."

"Tell me what you do know," I said, thinking about my own gut feeling that there was some connection, and Hensley Carroll's description of how he became Zrbny's attorney of record.

"She was one of the speakers at the neighborhood meeting that I mentioned. She and the Vigil guy had lunch together. The dining room was crowded, so we had to barge in on other groups where there were vacant seats. They were at a table for five. A colleague and I sat at their table. They were friendly enough, but it was apparent that we were intruding. They knew each other. That was obvious."

Pouldice had told me she did not know Fremont. Her people tried to interview him, she said. He would not talk to them. She had shot a glance at her Neanderthal, who was probably Hensley Carroll's big man bearing money.

"What about Donald Braverman?" I asked.

"The name doesn't mean anything to me."

I did a quick inventory of what I knew and what I suspected. Vigil was supposed to spring Felix Zrbny for BTT. That much was news-as-entertainment at its worst. Somewhere a line item on a production budget reflected the cost of liberating a multiple murderer. The more I considered that possibility, the more I felt what a short haul it was from reporting the news to creating it. The competition is fierce; the profits are staggering; and journalistic propriety leaves with the journalists. On TV the investigative reporters are replaced with personalities, voices, faces. As the line blurs between tabloid and traditional press, good reporters are replaced by diggers like Danny Kirkland, newshounds with fat budgets who are ready to print any unsubstantiated rumor or allegation. Their audience is prepared to gobble up whatever tale arrives on the tube or smells foul at the grocery checkout.

Simpson in Los Angeles. Ramsay in Boulder. Clinton-Lewinsky in the nation's capital. Zrbny in Boston.

Cary Stayner, the alleged killer of four in Yosemite National Park, was next in line to inherit the media mantle. Stayner was in his late thirties, handsome, rugged, in love with the outdoors. His confession to police, and his statement to a television reporter, included the near-decapitation of one of his victims and the decapitation of a second. It was the stuff of great media because it passed as news and spawned few complaints of violence during the family viewing hours. Everyone knows kids don't watch the news.

"You there, Lucas?"

"Just thinking. What about the Escher print?"

"*Relativity,*" Kelly said. "Felix doesn't want to talk about that any more than he will discuss his delusional activity, his 'lady of sorrow.' He had a copy of the print on his wall. He stared at it and seemed to enter a hypnoid state. If I or one of the staff spoke to him, he didn't respond, and I don't think he heard us."

"What about his voices?"

"Like I say, some topics were off-limits with him. He wouldn't go there, and he didn't want me to go there. I did some Internet research because that phrase, 'lady of sorrow,' sounded like a literary reference."

I remembered making my own association to Jean Genet.

"It's from Thomas De Quincey."

"*Confessions of an Opium Eater,*" I said, referring to the nineteenth-century writer's most famous prose poem.

"That's the guy. This piece is called *Levana and Our Ladies of Sorrow.*"

"His sister's name."

"I don't imagine De Quincey is where the Zrbnys came up with the name, but it is the same. Felix always used the singular, one lady. There are three in De Quincey, sisters. One for tears, one for sighs, one for darkness. I'm convinced that Escher and De Quincey are in his delusional mix, but I don't know the thought processes."

Tears, sighs, darkness. A trinity.

"Was his sister's disappearance the trigger? A couple of years to incubate, then he breaks out?"

"He did tell me about the day she vanished," Kelly said. "He never acknowledged this, but I always had the feeling that he witnessed her abduction."

Which would explain a lot of things, I thought. If Zrbny saw his sister grabbed, his pathology had an event around which to crystallize. He could also be Pouldice's unnamed source.

Kelly's parting suggestion was that I be sure to talk to the hospital attendant Ben Moffatt. "I think

Ben had a better relationship with Felix than any of the rest of us."

I thanked Kelly and hung up.

"Helpful?" Bolton asked.

"Very much so."

Kelly's information fit well with what I already knew, but it did not unlock the mysteries of Zrbny's mind. The killer had an agenda; I did not know it. He had moved on from the Riverway and the Towers; where was he? An army of police officers prowled the streets; no one saw Zrbny.

"Any word on Waycross?" I asked.

"Nothing."

"Did you ever figure out what he reacted to?"

He shook his head. "This is the file he was reading," he said, tossing it on the bed. "It's mostly lab reports."

"I'm gonna take a quick shower," I said. "I'll catch up with you at your office."

"You may have trouble getting there from here," he said. "It's still snowing."

. . . twenty inches of the white stuff has accumulated in the last twenty-four hours, and it's still snowing. Good morning. I'm Lily Nelson, and this is Boston Trial Television Headline News. We'll get to the weather story in just a moment, but first let's recap the events of what history will remember as the Bloodbath in Boston. The day started . . .

CHAPTER 24

AS I CLIMBED FROM THE LOFT, RALPH WAS heading for the door.

"Gotta do the linen," he said, ready to make his tour of the wards and units, distribute clean sheets and pillowcases and collect the dirty bedding. "After lunch I'll take a break. I'll bring some food."

I switched on the small TV.

"The police media relations department has scheduled a news conference for nine o'clock this morning," Lily Nelson said. "We'll be going to that live. In a related story, BTT's former news director and now the station's owner, Wendy Pouldice, is in seclusion at an undisclosed location. Early this morning, Ms. Pouldice had this to say about the carnage that has swept the city since Felix Zrbny's escape."

Pouldice stood at a lectern, gripping its edge with one hand and balling tissues with the other. "Bob Britton was a friend," she said, "not just an employee, but one of the best newscasters in the business, and a close, personal friend. He will be missed.

The sadness I feel, that all of us at Boston Trial Television feel, is immense and unremitting. In the wake of this bloodbath in Boston, we have become a city under siege."

"She is an actress," I said.

"In seclusion at an undisclosed location" meant her retreat on the Connecticut River near Claremont, New Hampshire. She had mentioned the place, her "big empty cave where I do nothing but watch the river flow."

When we talked during our visits, Pouldice seemed to understand what I wanted. I would give her exclusive rights to my story. I would answer all questions. She would give me my sister's killer.

She had waffled on my only demand. There was no way to be certain, she said. Seventeen years have passed, she said. Then, after her fourth visit, she called on the phone.

"I think I might have something," she said.

Pouldice told me about a girl named Theresa Stallings. "The kid was with a friend, playing basketball in Dorchester. A few days before she disappeared, a red-haired guy in a white car was hanging around the playground. He got out of the car, smoked, watched the kids play, got back in the car. It was like he was waiting. He had no reason to be there."

"Tell me about Theresa," I said.

"She was fifteen, tall for her age, dark hair, brown

eyes. She was wearing gray shorts and a Celtics shirt, thirty-three, Larry Bird's number."

I considered telling her where she could find Theresa. I did not.

"The man who took Theresa took my sister," I said.

"Felix, the abductions are six years apart. A white car? Who keeps a car six years, especially an American car? And a red-haired guy? Boston probably has more than most cities."

"Use your sources," I told her, and left it at that.

But I knew.

Now on TV, I watched a police captain named Newhall at a different podium, this one emblazoned with a police shield. "We've all had a rough twenty-four hours," he said. "It doesn't help that we've got the worst snowstorm since seventy-eight going on out there. This will work the way it always does. I can tell you some things, I can't tell you others."

He itemized the body count and was fairly accurate about who killed whom. They did not know the name of the man who killed Sable.

"We have eleven members of the group known as Vigil in custody," Newhall said. "Felix Zrbny remains at large at this time."

Newhall sounded like Broderick Crawford in Highway Patrol. At large. Ten-four. Cops on the alert. What did that mean? Cops are paid to be aware.

"*We have had no cooperation from Vigil. We have questioned the acknowledged leader of the group. Mr. John Jay Johnson, also known as J-Cubed, also known as Dermott Fremont, has refused to assist us with this investigation.*"

A small insert appeared on the screen, a file video of the man who was all Js. He was cuffed, and cops led him into a courthouse. He turned as he walked through the door. I saw him in profile—his prominent nose, his brush-cut red hair—precisely as I had seen him in his white car when he grabbed Levana.

RALPH RETURNED AT ONE P.M.

He fished through the large pocket that extended across the bottom of his sweatshirt. He produced rolls, slices of ham and cheese wrapped in a napkin, and a small piece of white cake.

"*If you don't want the cake,*" he said.

I pushed it across the small table to him, cracked open a roll and stuffed it with ham and cheese.

"*Marty Fenwick's got a pool going about when they catch you,*" Ralph said. "*Five dollars a date. The first ten days got covered right away. Only a couple of guys figure you'll last longer than that.*"

"*You want to make some money?*"

Ralph barked his short laugh. "*I got no money to make money with.*"

I reached into my pocket and pulled out a twenty

from Deputy Finneran's bills. "Make a side bet," I said. "Day after tomorrow."

"You ain't staying, Felix?"

"You want to go with me?"

"Oh Jesus no." *He stuffed cake into his mouth.* "I ain't going nowhere."

"It's like it was before, Ralph. I know what I have to do."

"They're gonna stick you in Walpole this time," *he cautioned.*

"I know who killed my sister," *I told him.* "I think I know why everything got so fucked up out there last night."

"You gotta make things right," *he said with a nod as tears formed in his eyes.* "You got to finish up."

"And you're going to make some money," *I said, tossing the twenty at him,* "maybe enough to get a new TV, one of those small color ones."

He yanked himself away from whatever he was thinking and switched on the TV. "I want to hear what they're saying before I go back to work."

I ate my makeshift sandwich.

"They're showing Riddle's Bar," *he said.*

I stuffed a second roll with ham and cheese and joined Ralph on the edge of the cot. "You know where that place is?" *I asked.*

"Terry used to go out eight stops on South Huntington, then she had to walk two blocks on Centre Street. I don't know what direction. There's J-Cubed."

This time the video showed Vigil's leader climbing out of a full-size white Ford and entering the bar. "He's bald," I said.

Ralph stared at the screen.

The next sequence showed Lucas Frank standing in front of my house. "Why did he go there?"

"To find out about you."

"Who's that with him?"

"An ex-cop named Waycross. You killed his wife, Felix. Don't you remember?"

"No," I said. "He looks nothing like he did fifteen years ago when he arrested me."

"He figure in this deal?"

"He did what he had to do."

"Felix, when are you going?"

"Tonight."

"It's still snowing out there. Jesus. Two feet and more coming."

"It slows down the world," I said. "Ralph, did you ever figure that maybe you should have been in Walpole?"

He shrugged. "The docs said I was crazy."

"Do you think you are?"

I could not tell whether Ralph was considering my question or immersing himself in the police press conference. "I think maybe I was," he said finally. "Now I think I'm just getting old."

I had questions about my own mind. "How do you think that cop feels?" I asked, pointing at Captain Newhall.

He hesitated. "He's doing his job."

"He sounds tired, maybe angry."

"He probably didn't get much sleep."

I tried a different approach. "When Terry used to visit, how did she feel about coming here?"

He continued to watch TV. "Sometimes she made good connections from the streetcar to the bus. Sometimes not so good. She didn't like the smell of this place. Mostly, she came and she went."

"Didn't it bother her to visit you here? Didn't she wish you were outside?"

"Nah. She always figured I'd get around to killing her."

CHAPTER 25

RAY BOLTON SAT AT HIS DESK. HE LOOKED as bad as I felt.

"There's coffee," he said.

I poured a cup and sat opposite him. "Stallings," I said.

"That's right. You wanted to look at the file."

He yanked open a drawer and hauled out two file folders. Combined, they were three inches thick. For an abduction and suspected homicide, that's nothing.

"This is it?"

"That's one of the reasons this case bothers me. Middle of the afternoon, sunny day, heavily populated area, plenty of traffic, pedestrians, a uniformed cop in a cruiser a block away, a furniture company repossessing a sofa across the street, and nobody saw anything."

I flipped open the top folder and paged through summary sheets until I found the case log. Each action taken during an investigation is entered chronologically in the log; officers append supplementary reports and exhibits later in the case file. The document has a language and shorthand all its own.

The R/O, reporting officer, was A. Hirsch, the first officer on the scene. "1500. Met by neighborhood residents (see list below), and witness, Margaret (Maggie) Winship, 13YO-F, W, Br/Br, 95, 5–3. V: Theresa M. Stallings, 15YO-F, W, Br/Br, 105, 5–6. APB radio, 1504. Assigned case number 0019438–88."

Hirsch's narrative followed. Maggie Winship was in shock, sitting in the middle of the basketball court surrounded by neighbors. It was just as Bolton had said. Winship could not talk, and nobody else had anything to talk about.

"The log doesn't include who called this in," I said.

"Adult female," Bolton said with a sigh. "She called on a direct line to one of the desks in Homicide. Never said who she was. There's a separate sheet later in the narrative."

The report of the initial event in this investigation appeared as an appended item, a one-paragraph afterthought.

"Why do you insist on calling this chronological case filing?"

"We've been through this, Lucas," he said.

"With the exception of the log, the sheets are appended when they're completed, not in accordance with the investigation's own timeline. I was looking at reports yesterday that had calls made from the Dayle residence days after she was dead, and from the Waycross residence hours after she was dead."

"I think the first time you pointed out log inconsistencies to me was twenty-five years ago in your kitchen."

"Didn't do any damn good," I grumbled, reading the one-paragraph insert. "Were these direct phone lines to the investigators' desks public information?"

"They're not in the book, but they're printed on our business cards."

"The location where she was grabbed is two blocks from Ashmont Station."

Bolton nodded. "Like I said, a heavily populated area."

"The detective who took the call, A. Garcia . . ."

"Andrea. She's with Baltimore P.D. now. The call came in on her line."

"Had she been investigating anything out there in the previous year?"

"I'd have to look it up. What are you getting at?"

"If she had a case that required her to be in Dorchester, and she conducted any interviews, she'd leave her card."

Bolton spun around to his computer, tapped the keys, and waited. "The Levesque shooting in May that year. Dorchester Avenue. That was Richard

Hamden's case. Let's see. Garcia assisted. They wrapped it in three days."

He attacked the keyboard a second time. "She talked to a dozen people out there."

"Work from Dorchester Avenue back to the playground," I suggested.

"It's got to be this one. Adele Robbins. Fuller Street. Lucas, this is one hell of a long shot."

"You want to clear the case, right?"

"You think there's a connection to Levana Zrbny."

I shrugged. "It's just a hunch."

I wish that I had kept count of the number of times I have flown by the seat of my pants. A hunch, intuition, a somewhat informed visceral sense of connectedness or meaning, often directed my work.

"I've got Vigil arraignments to deal with," Bolton said, "and it's still snowing. I can get to this in a couple of days."

"This is a mild winter at Lake Albert," I said, pushing myself from the chair. "If you don't have any objections, I'll head out to Dorchester."

"Wait. That reminds me."

He grabbed a sheet from his in-basket and pushed it across the desk. "That's a formal complaint," he said.

I skimmed the first few lines. "Who's William Hennesy?"

"He manages Riddle's Bar."

"Willy?" I read more. "I'm surprised. That's fairly accurate. I'll take care of this."

"Lucas, you're lucky that got kicked up to me. You have to respond to that in seven days."

"A misunderstanding," I said.

"Did you fire the gun?" Bolton's hands shot into the air. "Don't answer that."

"Willy and I will have a good chat over a couple of mugs of Guinness," I said, folding the complaint and stuffing it into my pocket. "You get anything on that second car parked at the courthouse?"

"Media," Bolton said.

"Fremont said there was a second car."

"That wasn't it. We have the plate number."

"Registered to whom?" I asked.

Bolton shuffled through papers. "I don't have it yet."

"Let me see it before you stuff it into your allegedly chronological file."

THE SNOW WAS HEAVIER THAN IT HAD BEEN the previous night, but the wind had died. Visibility and drifting were less problematic. Unlike many of the Dorchester side streets, a plow had visited Fuller Street.

Adele Robbins lived on the top floor of an asphalt-shingled three-story walk-up. The smell of eggs frying in butter greeted me in the hallway, grew stronger on the second floor, and faded on the third. I tapped on the door and waited, listening to TV noise from elsewhere in the building.

When the door opened, I looked down at a wizened, white-haired woman, less than five feet tall, weighing perhaps ninety pounds, and holding a cocked .44 caliber handgun.

She peered over the top of her half glasses and asked, "What the fuck do you want?"

I glanced from the weapon to her eyes, then back to the menacing artillery. "My name is Lucas Frank," I began.

"You didn't answer my question," she snapped.

"I want to ask you a few things about Theresa Stallings, the young girl—"

"I know who she is. You're no cop."

"I work with the police," I said quickly.

"Why'd it take you eleven years to get here?"

"You called Detective Garcia," I said.

"Of course I did. I told that twit what I saw out my window. She put down the phone and went off somewhere. That call was my damn dime. You got a gun?"

I do not recall a time when I have lost control of an interview so efficiently and quickly. "Yes," I said.

"Good. I got one, too. Mine's out and the hammer's back. You remember that."

"I will," I said, wondering what I had gotten myself into.

"Now you walk to that window and take a look,"

she said, backing into her apartment and pointing with her left hand.

Her living room was a virtual library of word puzzles—paper volumes of crosswords, anagrams, acrostics, cryptograms. Classical music drifted softly from her radio.

"May I push the curtain aside?" I asked.

"You can't see if you don't."

I looked at the playground—down forty feet, across an alley, and over a chain-link fence. "You saw what happened that day," I said.

"That's what I tried to tell the cop. Then I waited. They were going to different places on the street, asking questions. They never knocked on my door. That woman had been here before, asking me about a shooting on the avenue. She never came back."

"I'd like to know what you saw that day," I said.

"Now I'm gonna tell you that. Then you're gonna get out of here. I was sitting in that chair by the window, working on one of my mammoth crosswords. I needed a nine-letter word for wailing that started with a *C*."

"Caterwaul?"

"Smartass. I looked out when I heard the kids playing. That annoys some people but I like it, knowing the kids are out there with a basketball and not somewhere taking drugs. The red-haired bastard parked at the end of the alley. He'd been showing up for a week. I saw him do the same thing three times. He'd park, sit, get out of the car for a smoke, go back in, and the whole time he watched those little girls. The day it happened, he must've been following them, because he pulled in right after they got there. This time he didn't bother watching, he didn't have his smoke. He walked into that playground, grabbed the Stallings girl, dragged her to the car, and drove off. The whole thing was over in less than a minute."

Adele Robbins was telling me more than she realized. This guy had stalked Theresa Stallings, selected her ahead of time, and chose his location with care. He had done this before. Self-assured, confident, prepared—he was an experienced abductor.

"Can you describe him?" I asked.

"You waited eleven years to get here," Robbins said, "don't you get impatient with me. I don't guess heights, and I don't guess weights. Red hair I know when I see it. Cut short. He wore blue jeans every time I saw him. That last day, he had on a light blue shirt. Before you ask me about his car, I'm gonna tell you. White, like I said. They change so often, I don't know makes, but it was a big car, American, four doors. And before you ask me the license plate, I'm gonna give it to you."

She yanked open a drawer. I waited for her to produce a crumpled and yellowed slip of paper with a partial number. Instead, she lifted out a Massachusetts license plate.

"I didn't like the way he watched those kids," she said. "One day when he parked down there, I took my canvas shopping tote and a screwdriver and went out like I was doing my shopping. I crossed the street, went up a ways, then crossed back and came up behind the car. He was leaning against the front fender, smoking his cigarette, and I ducked down and took that off."

She gave me the plate. "You got three questions left, right?"

I looked at her. This was her show.

"Did I know who he was? Had I seen him before? Have I seen him since?"

I smiled. "That about covers it."

"I don't know who he was. I never saw him before. I saw him one time since, two years ago in Jamaica Plain. I was visiting my brother. I was on the bus and I saw him getting into a car on South Huntington Avenue. It was a white car, but not the same one I took that plate off. It happened real quick. His red brush cut was gone. He was bald."

"Am I allowed to thank you?" I asked.

"No. Just get the hell out."

THE CRIMINAL PSYCHIATRIC UNIT, A 1930S-vintage brick institution, loomed behind ominous stone walls topped with razor wire. I found the visitors' parking lot and hiked through the snow to the main entrance.

Although it is considered a treatment facility, CPU had the appearance and feel of a prison. The primary reasons for the unit's existence were to provide residential evaluations—what we used to call thirty- or sixty-day papers—of violent offenders to the courts, and to house those convicted of their offenses but deemed insane. I have never understood the distinction since one institution is much like another, and there were probably as many legally sane patients here as there were legally insane inmates in Walpole.

Six of one, half dozen of the other, I thought as the door clicked and I emerged from the locked sally port into a large, rectangular lobby.

I stopped to allow a determined young man in bathrobe, pajamas, and slippers to pass. He stopped abruptly, shouted "Nelson," thumped himself soundly on his chest with both fists, then continued his focused trek across the lobby.

I headed for a cubicle that housed the only other person in sight.

Her nameplate said she was Beck. Short for Rebecca? Or Ms. Beck? She wore a pink volunteer's smock and was close in age, but fortunately not disposition, to my friend Adele Robbins.

"I saw you on *Unsolved Mysteries*," Beck said, before I could speak.

"I wasn't the fugitive they were hunting," I said.

She laughed.

"I'm Lucas Frank. I called this morning and left

a message for Ben Moffatt. He should be expecting me."

"Let's see. Ben's on Ward 6. Just a moment."

She punched buttons on her phone, waited, punched more, then delivered her message. "He'll be right down," she said. "It's just terrible about Felix Zrbny. I never met him. We aren't allowed on the wards, and even if we were, I wouldn't go there. Some of the attendants referred to him as the Gentle Giant. Not so gentle, I'd say."

The man in the bathrobe made another pass. "Nelson." Thump, thump.

Ben Moffatt emerged from a door marked Restricted Access.

"Dr. Kelly suggested that I talk with you," I said.

"I don't know what I can tell you that he can't," Moffatt said, directing me to one of the many vinyl sofas in the waiting area.

"I'm trying to understand how Felix Zrbny thinks, how his delusions are expressed in his behavior. If I can accomplish that, I might be able to come up with an idea where he is, perhaps narrow the search a bit."

"Wow," Moffatt said, pushing his hands through his hair. "I don't know how he thinks. Felix is a bright, complex man. Did Dr. Kelly tell you about the Escher print?"

I nodded. "And the lady of sorrow, the De Quincey reference. I have no idea how any of that fits together, and I don't understand the role that his sister's disappearance plays in all this."

"Levana," he said. "When Mrs. Zrbny committed suicide, her husband was totally overwhelmed. People usually bounce back after a tragedy. There's a healing process, then they try to put a life together. He couldn't do that. Felix and Levana took care of each other. She was older, so mostly she looked after him, but he did his share of the cooking, washing dishes, laundry. They were friends. He'd always been a loner. Levana was more outgoing. She led. He followed."

"Ben," Beck called. "Ralph's coming through with the laundry cart."

Moffatt excused himself, unlocked the door, and crossed the lobby with a short, one-armed man pushing a laundry bin. Moffatt unlocked then secured the second door.

"D-wing," he called to Beck as he returned and settled into the sofa. "The day Levana was abducted—"

"You sound certain of that."

"I don't think Felix ever lied to me. He withheld. If I asked him a direct question that he didn't want to answer, he just didn't. One time when he was talking about Levana, I said, 'You saw her grabbed, didn't you?' He sat there stone-faced."

"He might have had the same response if he had killed his sister."

Moffatt shrugged. "Maybe, but I don't see it happening that way. I think he blamed himself for what happened. The next couple of years it gnawed at him. He needed someone in his life. There was no one. That's when he became obsessed with the Escher print. He saw it as a finite world with infinite unrealized possibilities. That's a quote. If people shared space, but on different planes, they couldn't see or touch each other. He knew his victims. He believed that not only did they not know him, but that they refused to see him. When he stumbled across the De Quincey passage, his delusional system crystallized. Levana is the mythical force that inspires and empowers a family member to present a newborn child to the world. Then Levana watches as the child develops, and pays special attention to a child who is grieving."

"Felix was in grief over his sister," I said, catching Moffatt's direction.

"Levana's ladies of sorrow were tears, sighs, and darkness."

It was the same thing Kelly had told me.

"Tears," Moffatt said. "He told me about walking out of a classroom in high school. Gina Radshaw was outide the door crying. He tried to talk to her, to see if there was anything he could do to help. She never looked at him. She ran out of the building. His lady of tears."

"And someone who could not, or did not see him," I suggested.

"You're catching on. Florence Dayle needed help turning a faucet that was stuck. She led Felix into the cellar. He said she sighed these huge, breathy sighs, as if she were impossibly sad. She never looked at him. When he had done what she asked, she told him to leave."

"Shannon Waycross was dark skinned."

"Our lady of darkness. She hid behind sunglasses, said she didn't want the newspaper Felix was selling."

Moffatt was able to see the significance of themes in Zrbny's life. Approach; a service offered or provided; rejection.

"What tipped him?" I asked.

"Radshaw worked in his neighborhood. Waycross and Dayle lived there. No one of them knew any of the others. When Radshaw left work, she walked past both of the other women's houses. They were next-door neighbors, but they didn't know one another, and neither knew Radshaw."

"Escher," I said.

Moffatt smiled. "Some docs are slow to catch on. You're okay."

"Why would Zrbny say he'd been interrupted?" I asked. "There are three ladies of sorrow. He killed three times."

"I wondered about that. I wouldn't describe Felix as rigid exactly, but his thinking is ordered. Even at his most delusional he is organized. Sorry. I can't do the math on that one."

"Is there any reality referent for the Escher print?" I asked.

"Maybe," he said. "Felix told me about the dungeons at the top of Ravenwood. It's an old fort that was used in both World Wars to watch the coast for the enemy. The area is fenced off now because the field that surrounds it is riddled with sinkholes and old wells. There's a lookout tower and hundreds of yards of underground corridors and cells. I don't know how it fits, but I think that's the piece of reality in his delusions."

"When I visited his home, I found a copy of the print with a photograph taped to the middle of it."

Moffatt smiled. "Wendy Pouldice?"

"How did you know?"

"Think about it. She's the eyes for all of us. She's at the center watching what others can't see or don't want to see. Then she has her stories for TV. She visited Felix a number of times."

My young man in the bathrobe halted his journey six feet from us, yelled "Nelson," and thumped himself. He performed a ninety-degree turn with military precision.

"Schizophrenic," I said.

"He has been with us three months. His meds are still not regulated."

"Why does he have to jump-start his heart so often?"

"Do you know Paul Nelson?"

"Haven't had the pleasure. Do you mind?"

I followed Nelson until he came to a stop and completed his ritual. "Mr. Nelson, may I inspect your battery?" I asked.

Nelson yanked open his bathrobe and displayed a smashed Walkman clipped to his pajamas. The tape player lacked covers for its battery compartment and tape housing.

"May I?" I asked, pointing at his "battery."

He slipped it from his waistband and handed it to me. I examined it carefully.

"I see two choices," I said. "We can recharge this battery, or we can replace it. What would you prefer, Mr. Nelson?"

"Recharge," he snapped, and waggled his fingers in front of his face. "Recharge and charge it."

I opened my pocketknife's screwdriver blade, poked and probed at the black plastic box, yanked out the knife's corkscrew and scraped what was left of the tape heads, then returned it to Nelson.

"Good as new," I said. "I'll put it on your account. I think you'll find that these adjustments will allow you to complete your journey."

"Recharge and charge it," he said again, clipping the Walkman in place and surging across the lobby.

"Who is his therapist?" I asked, returning to the sofa.

"He's been evaluated," Moffatt said. "He hasn't been assigned."

"Whoever gets him will need a pocketknife, and

a ledger card for Nelson's account. He'll be manageable, and when his meds are adjusted you should see some improvement. Where were we?"

Moffatt smiled. "I wish you worked here," he said. "We were talking about Boston's own Barbara Walters."

"Right. We left her in the middle of Escher, didn't we?"

"I asked Felix if he knew Pouldice fifteen years ago. It was one of those times that he didn't answer."

I watched Nelson cruise the lobby without breaking stride. "Does he have any hope of release?" I asked.

"None. He was a preacher in one of those off-the-map religions. He became convinced that his wife and two kids were inhabited by the devil."

"So he killed them."

"Then dismembered them looking for Satan. Somebody called the cops when the parsonage started to smell bad."

"What did he do with their hearts?"

"The cops never found the hearts," Moffatt said, walking me to the sally port.

"If Nelson has the devil on his tail," I said, paraphrasing the Robert Johnson song, "he's going to need that battery in tip-top condition."

I thanked Moffatt for his help and waited for the various electronic doors to click me back into

Boston's winter. Danny Kirkland was there to greet me.

"Where's Brother Waycross today?" he asked.

I ignored him.

"I'm getting tired of the fuckin' snow," he said.

"I'm tired of you," I told him, walking to my car.

Kirkland tagged along. "I'm gonna give you more than I should," he said. "A sample, a preview of coming attractions."

"Where's my popcorn?"

"Funny, Doc. Zrbny says he was interrupted fifteen years ago, right?"

I continued walking.

"He knew who he was gonna kill before he went out that afternoon."

I stopped at my car.

"Tell me I'm wrong."

I waited.

"So he knows who he didn't kill, right?"

"Get to the profound insight part," I said.

He shrugged. "I ain't got that part because I haven't seen the fuckin' reports."

"Got a theory?"

"Shit yes, I have a theory. That's where the sharing comes in. Out of all those boxes in your hotel room, there's maybe six pieces of paper I gotta see. The theory holds water or it don't. Either way I tell you."

My impulse was to dismiss Kirkland and his

theory, but he wrestled with the same conundrum that gnawed at me. Zrbny had sought and found and killed his requisite trinity of ladies and then, he said, Waycross had interrupted him.

"I'll think about it," I said, climbing into the Ford and driving off.

CHAPTER 26

RALPH PUSHED OPEN THE DOOR TO HIS bedroom-storage area. He was early.

"That shrink who was on TV is sitting in the lobby talking to Ben Moffatt," Ralph said. "It's weird to see someone on TV and then see him for real."

"He isn't just digging up background on me," I said. "He's tracking me."

"You ain't worried?"

Two hours earlier a TV bio had described Lucas Frank as an expert on violent behavior, a retired psychiatrist and independent profiler. Originally from Boston, he now lived in the Michigan woods. They also reported that he had been accused of discharging a firearm in Riddle's Bar. In some strange parallel way, he was as thorough as I, and appeared to share some of the same goals.

"He won't find me until I'm ready to be found," I told Ralph.

"You gonna kill him?"

I ignored the question because I did not know the answer.

"Felix, do you know why I killed the hot dog vendor at Fenway Park?" Ralph asked. "I broke my fingernail trying to open the fuckin' little package of mustard. It hurt like a bastard. Ah, I was pissed off at the Red Sox anyway."

"You shot him?"

"Then half the bleachers piled on me, but I almost got away. That's important. There were so many guys piled on me, they didn't know who was who. I squirmed out, but there was a cop there by then. Felix, will I see you again?"

"I don't know," I told him.

BREAKING OUT OF THE HOSPITAL PROVED to be easier than breaking in.

The snow had tapered to flurries, and the wind had stopped. Evening personnel were in the building; day staff had gone. No guards wandered the grounds with flashlights.

I crossed the yard to where my maple branch extended over the razor wire and hung down with the weight of the snow. I jumped, grabbed the lowered branch, and hoisted myself into the tree.

I crawled the length of the branch to the trunk, then dropped to the ground. Traffic was light as I jogged the sidewalk to Jamaica Plain.

There were four cars—three of them buried in drifts—in Riddle's parking lot. I looked through the restaurant window. One man leaned on the bar and watched TV. J-Cubed sat huddled with three men at a rear table. The restaurant section was empty.

I waded through the snow, testing windows and doors on the side of the building. At the back a wooden platform led to a flight of stairs and a door. Its glass panel had long ago been replaced with plywood and hardware cloth, and it was secured with rotting planks. I ripped away the boards and leaned against the door, shoving until nails squealed loose and the door opened.

Riddle's storage area contained cases of beer and whiskey piled to the ceiling. I moved slowly among cartons of napkins and peanuts, crates of relish, mustard, and salsa. There was another door, unlocked, that opened on the hallway to the men's room. People who drink, I reasoned, must eventually visit the bathroom, so I slipped into the cracked-tile, piss-stinking room and waited.

The day that I stood on Ridge Road and watched Levana disappear into the white car, I chased after them. The driver made the big curve and drove farther up the hill. I wondered where he was going; I had never seen that car on the hill. When he turned onto the road that led to the dungeons, I ran into the woods and climbed to the field near the lookout tower. I did not see the car, and I did not see my sister.

I ran across the meadow to the pullout where kids parked to make out. No one was there. The soft hiss of the breeze through the long grass was the only sound I heard. I turned and ran to one of the three entrances to the dungeons.

As I watched the image of myself step inside the concrete bunker—nearly as if I saw it on a TV screen—Riddle's bathroom door opened. The man who walked to the urinal was slightly built, in his thirties, and bald like the rest of Vigil's legions.

I stood on the toilet seat and reached down, grabbing him around the throat with my forearm. He struggled briefly, squirmed, kicked the stall. When he was unconscious, I dropped him, dragged his limp form into the stall, and broke his neck. The vertebral crunch of his spine echoed in the small bathroom.

In minutes a second man entered. "Newt? Where the fuck did you go?"

Newt's friend, and then another, heightened my pile of corpses. Now I waited only for J-Cubed.

"What the fuck are you guys doing, jerking each other off?" he demanded, shoving open the bathroom door.

I grabbed him by the shirt collar and his belt, and slammed him against the tile wall. He crumpled to the floor. I lifted him and sat him in the sink, relieving him of a handgun and a Buck knife. Then I waited the few moments until he groaned his way to semiconsciousness.

"What do you want?" he mumbled.

He reached up and tenderly touched his bloody

face. "You broke my nose. What the fuck are you doing?"

I waited for his head to clear, for him to see me, to recognize me.

My cue was when he focused his eyes and said, "Oh Jesus no."

"You talk," I said. "I listen."

"I don't have anything to say."

I pushed open the stall door and allowed him to view his stack of dead friends.

"Fuck. You're gonna kill me anyway."

"If you don't talk to me, I'll break you bone by bone."

"What do you want to know?"

"Start with my sister, Levana Zrbny. Seventeen years ago you dragged her into your car in Raven-wood. You took her to the old fort at the top of the hill."

"No."

I stuffed paper towels into his mouth. His eyes widened and he gagged.

I gripped the sink with my right hand, grabbed his wrist with my left, and yanked his elbow hard against my right forearm. He tried to lurch from the sink, but he was too slow. It was like ripping apart a turkey wing and glancing briefly at the exposed bone while you decide where to bite.

I slapped my hand across his mouthful of paper and held it there, muffling his roar of pain. Tears *streamed from his eyes and flowed across the back of my hand. His arm dangled uselessly.*

When he only whimpered and wept, I removed my hand, picked out the towels that he had not swallowed, and said again, "You talk. I listen."

"I saw her on the road," he began, gasping his words like Mrs. Dayle had. "I'd seen her before."

CHAPTER 27

BOLTON HAD JUST RETURNED FROM COURT. "I'll be ecstatic when I don't have to do this anymore," he grumbled, loosening his necktie. "You talk to William Hennesy?"

"Not yet," I said.

"Lucas, that complaint is no joke."

"I said I'll take care of it. Right now it's low on my list of things to do."

I gave Bolton the old license plate that Adele Robbins had given me.

"What the hell is this?"

"If you can find out who had that plate eleven years ago, you can close Stallings and quit."

Bolton stared at me.

I told him about Adele, her theft of the license plate, and her witnessing Theresa Stallings's abduction while working on a mammoth crossword. "She needed 'caterwaul' and she says your response time sucks."

Bolton did not say a word. He took the plate and walked out of his office.

"I'm not finished," I yelled after him.

I leaned back in my chair and allowed my eyes to close. The noise—voices, fingers tapping keyboards, phones whining, a door slamming—faded. Ben Moffatt's words formed a visual tapestry, a banner announcing "a finite world with infinite unrealized possibilities."

I saw the words drift by, and I felt empty, confused.

Limited, but with unlimited potential.

Poets know more about life than shrinks, and they express what they know in pleasant rhythms without numbers.

Possibilities unrealized. Infinite.

> *at the crazy house on Halloween, the kids*
> *   wore*
> *masks and went trick-or-treating . . .*
> *all the other days of the year the kids wore*
> *masks, and lived without chocolate bars*

What are you about, lad? You are forever behind your mask, banging around in your stone hallways, waiting. What are you waiting for?

I had looked into Felix Zrbny's eyes, and I had seen only determination there. There was no life in those eyes.

> *are your dreams insane, too?*
> *do you spin and mumble in sleep,*

*speak in rhyme, wear clothing backwards
and disregard time?*

Each of us has a representational system, a preferred way of absorbing and describing the world. A kid from the country who visits the city might describe the noise, the incessant din emitted by a million people. Her dominant manner of experiencing her world is auditory. Someone else might report odors, the strange blend of a breeze from the harbor and the city's exhaust.

Felix Zrbny knew the world visually.

The M. C. Escher print that hung on his bedroom wall and that Zrbny "disappeared" into was a two-dimensional representation of multiple dimensions.

Similar to TV, isn't it, lad?

Edmund Kemper complained that his victims were aloof, not involved with him. He wanted a relationship, he said. The only way he knew to achieve his goal was to kill them. Kemper's notion of relationship did not include give-and-take. He wanted their recognition, he wanted to control them, to be more than a passing participant in their lives. He would own them as completely as another person can be owned, by killing them.

At the age of fourteen, Felix Zrbny was powerless. Levana was gone, and his world was empty.

You saw Gina Radshaw and Shannon Waycross and Florence Dayle drift by one another—day after day. Each inhabited her own dimension and you watched them all. None of them saw you. They were supposed to comfort you in your grief, weren't they? Tears, darkness, and sighs—emissaries from Levana—your lady of sorrow. You crawled into the picture and took ownership of their lives.

"Where does TV come into it?" I asked.

Zrbny had to be the one who called Pouldice. He told her what he was going to do before he left his house. Pouldice had reported Levana Zrbny's abduction. She blasted the cops and made her own news. She became the media voice for Boston's lost and stolen children.

Theresa Stallings was next.

Pouldice made her own news.

Zrbny had shown no interest in being released from the hospital. She visited him, they exchanged numerous phone calls, then he wanted out.

Neville Waycross interrupted you. Your business was unfinished.

"Three is three, damn it," I muttered.

Bolton walked into the office and sat on the edge of his desk.

"I didn't have to ask you to run that old plate, did I?" I asked.

He said nothing.

"J-Cubed," I said. "What have you got on his North Carolina arrests?"

"We're pulling them now."

"Were you able to preserve any standards?"

"We have hairs from Theresa's brush."

"If the car hasn't been junked, can you find it?" I asked, thinking that a thorough forensic examination of the vehicle might still produce a hair or two for comparison.

"I've got an officer working on it."

I pushed myself from the chair and walked to the door.

"Lucas, what does this have to do with Zrbny?"

"You'll have to work Mr. Cubed," I said. "I think he grabbed Levana Zrbny. I also think there's a connection between that bald bastard and Pouldice, and we know she got herself in tight with Zrbny."

"So, why did Zrbny suddenly decide he wanted out?"

"Maybe Wendy Pouldice led him to J-Cubed," I said. "If that's the case, you'd best pick him up before Zrbny gets to him."

I walked to the door. "One other thing," I said. "Have you had any recent dealings with Danny Kirkland?"

"No," he said emphatically.

"He's been following me around. Says he has a theory about what went down fifteen years ago."

"We know what happened that day."

"We don't know who else Zrbny had targeted," I said. "Waycross interrupted him."

"Kirkland knows?"

I shrugged. "I'm sure I'll stumble over him again."

I HEADED FOR THE HOTEL TO CATCH UP ON my sleep and to grab something to eat. After that, I would try again to talk with Ms. Pouldice.

I was exhausted. My head touched the pillow and I was gone. There was no Cecil B. DeMille epic this time, no cast of dozens, no sound, no fury. Still, I slept only twenty minutes, then snapped to attention in bed in the darkened room.

"Fuck," I bellowed, grabbing the TV remote and slamming buttons.

I had not watched what remained of Severance's interview with Zrbny. He had been telling his tale of the goats and the troll modified for him by his sister.

"Then what?" Severance asked.

"I killed her."

"You said nothing to her?"

"She never saw me, why would she hear me? I didn't exist for her."

"Felix, how many times did you stab this young woman?"

"Three, four."

Severance hesitated and glanced at his notes. "Gina Radshaw was stabbed fifty-one times."

"How many times was Levana stabbed?" Zrbny asked.

Again, Severance paused briefly. "Your sister vanished. She was never found. Were you seeking vengeance?"

Zrbny did not respond.

"Did you kill those women because your sister was gone, taken from you?"

"That's the sort of question that you're supposed to answer," Zrbny said.

"Do you remember stabbing Gina Radshaw after she was dead?"

"I know what I did."

Severance sighed. "When you feel angry, what is it like? What is your experience of that feeling?"

Zrbny was silent.

"For someone to stab another person so many times . . ."

"That's what you believe."

"Help me to understand what you believe."

Zrbny continued to stare at Severance, his body rigid. "Someone should have asked me that a long time ago. I intend to remain here. What difference does it make? You will write a report and nothing will change."

Severance looked helpless.

"I'm a case, a file, a pile of papers. Add yours to the stack."

Zrbny stood and walked out of camera range. The tape ended.

Something got you moving in a different direction, lad.

I grabbed the phone and stared at the instructions for making a call. I put on my glasses and read the damn thing. How the fuck was I supposed to know whether I was making a local call? I punched the number for the desk. The young man who answered had mastered the Boston version of the British accent. He sounded as if he had a large growth under his tongue, and feared to part his lips because he might expose the mass.

"Place this call for me," I said.

"I'm sorry, sir. We don't do that from here. If you consult the hotel services manual provided—"

"What do you do in an emergency?"

He stalled only momentarily. "Call 911."

"If you can do that from there, you can do this." I gave him Pouldice's number.

"Sir . . ."

"Would you rather continue sounding like Surrey, or should I come down there and knock you back into Southie?"

"Just a moment."

The effort was a waste of time. No one answered.

Severance had conveyed his bias that rage was a necessary component when a killer stabs a victim fifty-one times. Zrbny did not share that bias. I wondered if, like many other killers, Zrbny split away his feelings, dissociated, or if he was something different—not unique, but rare—an emotional primitive who simply did what he believed needed to be done.

A delusional psychopath.

Severance asked how many times Zrbny stabbed Gina Radshaw.

"Three, four."

Was the response deceptive? Was he unaware? Or did he just not give a shit?

"How many times was Levana stabbed?"

As I dressed I considered Zrbny's linking the two young women's deaths.

"Did you kill those women because your sister was gone, taken from you?" Severance had asked.

Severance did what any shrink would do: he accepted the metaphor, the implied meaning.

I sat down hard on the bed.

That was not a metaphor, was it, lad? You know how many times your sister was stabbed.

I grabbed my coat and ran for the door.

The next twenty seconds—from when I yanked open the door until I told the fraudulent Brit kid from Southie to call 911—were like a nightmare ripped from Stephen King's notebook.

I froze in the doorway, trying to understand a Halloween prank in January.

The puddle of gore was no trick.

On the floor, staring vacantly skyward, was Dermott Fremont's head.

CHAPTER 28

I CAUGHT A RIDE WITH A TRUCKER HEADING west on the Massachusetts Turnpike. He was a small, wiry man—a younger version of Ralph Amsden, I thought—and a talker.

"I'm meeting some buddies at a truck stop outside of Springfield," he said. "One of them's driving a flatbed north. He'll get you close to Claremont."

I thanked him and watched highway crews with bucket loaders and dump trucks clearing the tons of snow.

"Hell of a storm," he said. "Don't usually see this kind of snowfall here. Colorado maybe, or up in the Sierras."

He did not seem to mind that I had little to say. He was content to have company, an audience for his stories.

His friend was a squat, heavyset trucker named Gary Baylor. The two men shared stories for an hour in the truck stop, then Baylor and I climbed into the cab of his flatbed and drove north.

I was twelve when my sister disappeared into

Fremont's white car and I followed, running up the hill to the dungeons. I stood inside the entrance and heard water dripping—like the soft tap of tears falling into their own shallow pool. As I moved deeper into the concrete bunker, the afternoon sunlight faded and the darkness swallowed me. I heard breathing, as if someone sighed deeply, far ahead in the tunnel or on a different level or on the other side of the wall.

My body shook, vibrated like a plucked strand of taut wire. Terror would not allow me to speak, to call my sister's name, to scream. I knew the dungeons, their secret passages, water-filled holes, rat-infested crevices, and corridors that went nowhere.

"You been up this way before?" Baylor asked.

"I've never been out of Massachusetts."

"It's nice country. Can't see much of it now."

"There doesn't seem to be as much snow here," I said.

"The storm veered off the coast. Boston and New York got hammered. It's even worse around D.C."

We drove in silence for a few moments, then Baylor said, "If you're coming up here looking for work, you won't have any trouble finding it. None of the jobs pay much, though."

"I have to see someone."

"Girlfriend?"

"A woman I had an agreement with."

"She jump off the seesaw, did she? Shit. I'm on my fourth wife. I don't know anything more about women now than I did when I was in high school."

Baylor's tale of his aborted marriages and flawed wives consumed the miles. I thought of Wendy Pouldice.

My father was in church the first time she knocked on the door. "He won't talk to you," I told her. "He doesn't talk to me."

Her smooth skin, bright blue eyes, and gentle smile were framed by a shoulder-length fall of soft blond hair. "Maybe you and I should talk," she said. "You hungry? How about a burger and fries?"

"I'm not supposed to go out."

She considered that. "When will your dad be home?"

"He goes to the cemetery after church. He visits my mother's grave."

"Will he be gone another hour?"

"A little longer."

"We have plenty of time. I'll have you back before he gets here, and he won't even know you were gone."

Much later, when Pouldice tried to talk to my father, he was polite, but he refused. She visited me only when he was at his shop. She wanted to help, she told me.

"I will find out who did this to Levana," she said.

"The police said she probably ran away."

"I don't believe that for a second. Do you?"

I hesitated, then shook my head.

"Tell me what you think happened," she said, and eventually I did.

Now, the truck slowed. "Exit eight," Baylor said. "I'll drop you at a store down there. I gotta fill my thermos."

"Which way is Claremont?"

"East," he said. "It's a long walk. This time of night there isn't much traffic, and it's a hell of lot colder than where we came from."

"Is there a motel near here?"

"The City Line. When you cross the bridge, it's on your right."

I thanked Baylor, flipped up my coat collar, shoved my hands into my pockets, and headed east.

A pink neon sign with most of its letters illuminated announced the City Line Motel. A hand-painted board nailed to a picket fence advertised cable TV and hot showers. Two other makeshift signs read Vacancies and No Pets.

My room was the last in a row of a dozen in a low, wood-frame building. I sprawled on the bed, unwrapped a sandwich I'd bought from the night clerk, and grabbed the TV remote. Suddenly I had no interest in what they were saying about me. I dropped the remote and bit into my Italian cold cuts on a bulkie roll.

When Fremont's tears had cascaded across the back of my hand, I flashed on the rivulets of condensation inside my refrigerator, and on an image of myself sitting on the kitchen floor feeling the cool air and watching the water flow across well-worn plastic paths. I listened for the sound of the water,

*but I heard only the whisper of Wendy Pouldice's TV
voice.*

*I could not call her then. She was on the air, alive
in my TV. When I was ready—when I was clear in
my mind about what I would do—then I would tell
her.*

*Wendy, I would say, imagining her in a night-
gown standing on her bed watching Mary Martin,
then soaring into the air, flitting around the room,
and flying through her window into the night.
Wendy, I'm ready to show you what I saw. I'm going to start by cutting my way through the darkness. Bring your camera. Then I will put an end to
the tears and silence and sighs, and my sister can
sleep.*

*Wendy Pouldice would arrive with her camera
crew and microphones. "This is 'Local Scene' with
Wendy Pouldice, live from Ravenwood, where . . ."*

*Dermott Fremont had required considerably less
persuasion to tell me his Wendy Pouldice story than
to talk about my sister. Waiting for Ms. Local Scene
to return from New Hampshire at her leisure was
out of the question. She would return with me.*

*I bit into my sandwich and stared at the blank TV
screen.*

. . . nationwide manhunt, but the search focus is the greater Boston area. Boston police are being assisted in their effort by the FBI and the United States Marshals. A source close to the investigation told BTT just moments ago that police are confident they will apprehend Felix Zrbny, and that they expect to find the mass murderer here in the city. Informants continue to report sighting Zrbny, who at six feet seven inches tall and nearly three hundred pounds should be hard to miss or to confuse with most other men his age. He is twenty-nine, has shoulder-length black hair and brown eyes. Zrbny is known to be armed and should be considered extremely dangerous. When we come back, we are going to recap . . .

CHAPTER 29

"THREE MORE DEAD IN THE BATHROOM AT Riddle's," Bolton said as crime scene technicians worked in the hall outside my door. "All Vigil members. Zrbny broke their necks."

"He waited for them."

"That's what it looks like. He stacked them like sacks of grain."

"He wanted J-Cubed. If Zrbny had to kill a dozen to get this one, he would have."

"Why do you get the head?"

"Both ears and the tail," I muttered, thinking that Zrbny was more than a step ahead of me. "He's watching us on TV. He knows who I am, why I'm here, the information I'm working with. He has the same information, but he obtained most of his firsthand. I think he saw Fremont kill his sister. Or maybe he saw her after Fremont was finished with her. He spent fifteen years putting it together. At the end, Pouldice was the catalyst."

"The plate on the car in the courthouse alley came back to BTT. The station had a crew of two on the front steps. They had their own van. Braverman had the car."

"He left the airport as soon as I got there," I said. "He had plenty of time. Everyone was on schedule except Zrbny. He spoiled the party."

I wondered if Zrbny knew the plans for his escape from the courthouse, then wondered if he had made the connection between Vigil and BTT.

I grabbed my coat. "I have to talk to Pouldice," I said.

"Her office says she's in seclusion. I sent two units to the Towers to bring in Braverman. He's disappeared. Pouldice has an estate on the Connecticut River in New Hampshire. That's where she is."

"Braverman with her?"

"The office manager, Hannah Stanley, didn't think so. She said Pouldice has always gone there alone."

"You got a home phone for Hannah?"

Bolton flipped through his notebook and gave me the number.

"If I find Braverman, I'll bring him back," I said.

"Preferably alive, Lucas. Right now we have questions. That's it."

"I assure you that I will do my best to preserve his anatomical integrity."

BOLTON KNEW ONLY THAT POULDICE'S second home was near Claremont. I stopped in the hotel lobby, grimaced at the phone, then called Hannah, the BTT office manager.

"Sorry to drag you from sleep at this hour," I said.

"I remember you," Hannah mumbled.

"Wendy has been overwhelmed by the last two days," I said. "I have to leave in the morning, and I want to FedEx something to her in New Hampshire, but I need the street address."

"I'm not supposed to give that out, Dr. Frank, and I can't reach her to ask her. Her cell phone is switched off, and the land lines are down from the storm. I tried all evening to call her."

"I'm sure this one exception would please her, Hannah. Wendy and I go back a lot of years. You know that. When we had dinner two nights ago, I promised that I would not leave the city before I gave her this small package. We had no way to foresee events."

Hannah considered her options. "She did seem eager to see you."

She gave me the address.

I glanced at the wall clock behind the desk. Allowing extra time for bad roads, I could reasonably expect to be in Claremont by six A.M. I found my way out of the city and drove north.

Road conditions improved outside Boston. When I reached Concord, New Hampshire, and picked up I-89, steep snowbanks lined the highway, but the pavement was clear. Northern New

England is prepared to deal with heavy snowfall. Days would pass before the Boston area approached anything resembling normal, whatever that was.

I left the interstate at the Lake Sunapee exit and drove west. Near Bradford, five deer descended an embankment on my right, crossed the road, and disappeared into the woods on the left. I felt homesick for Lake Albert.

The dashboard clock read 6:35 when I pulled into downtown Claremont. The lights were on at Daddy Pops Humble Inn, a diner tucked between a row of stores and a dozen dead factories. I had heard of the diner on an earlier trip north. What it lacked in exterior appearance—it looked like a retired city bus—Daddy Pops more than made up for with excellent food at reasonable prices.

Music played softly from a wooden radio with a cloth-covered speaker—nothing but tunes from the fifties and sixties, and no advertising. I sipped coffee and waited for my eggs and home fries. The front page of a local newspaper was thumbtacked to the wall behind the counter. The headline, INCINERATOR WOES, hyped the hot topic of the day, a controversial trash-burning facility. I doubted that the six-page paper contained a word about the "Bloodbath in Boston."

When the cook delivered my breakfast and a coffee refill, I asked him about Pouldice's rural route address.

"That's west," he said. "Go like you're going to Vermont. Just before the bridge, take your right. The way the letters and numbers work, this should be a dirt road on your left maybe a mile north."

Twenty minutes later I was back on the road following his directions. At first, route 12A swung away from the river; at a half mile, it veered back to the west. There were two dirt roads. I chose the one with the Private Property No Trespassing sign.

The mailbox displayed the correct rural route address. The private road wound through a snow-laden evergreen forest that opened on a clearing dominated by an expansive white house. I parked in front of the open garage and walked slowly to the porch, glancing in windows as I went.

Pouldice's condo in the Towers was stark, post-modern—a collage of white hemp, black leather, and natural wood slapped together from an interior designer's nightmares. This house had evolved, accepting additions through nearly two hundred years.

When no one responded to my knock on the front door, I tried the handle. It was locked. I retreated to the garage and found its interior door open. I stepped inside and moved slowly from a mudroom into the main hall.

The house was silent. I walked slowly through the hall, peering into rooms as I went. Pouldice's study was a large, bright room on the east side of the house. Four windows offered views of a

peaceful, snow-covered field, a scene in sharp contrast with the study's condition. The place had
been ransacked.

I continued through the hall until I reached the
oversized entryway.

I saw the gun first, a magnum, resting on a
black and crimson Persian carpet. Two feet beyond
the gun was an inert Donald Braverman, a single
black hole in his forehead.

CHAPTER 30

THE DREAM WAS REAL, FILLED WITH THE TEX-
tures, odors, and images of my world when I was
fourteen years old.

My T-shirt was soaked with sweat as I stepped from
the August heat into the cool, dark, damp dungeon. A
muffled scream echoed somewhere deep inside the
concrete corridors. I walked into the blackness that I
knew so well. I avoided the deep pools of stagnant water, fingered my way along the wall, listened, and
moved forward, staring into endless night.

I stood enveloped by darkness and listened to a
long, deep sigh. The slow erosion of the walls by
moisture, the dripping of water into accumulations
of itself, grew faint. A new trickling thundered from
the black recesses ahead of me. I was certain that I
heard the sound of my sister's tears, but when I
reached her side, I knew.

I had heard Levana's last breath, and the blood
drain from her body.

I opened my eyes, surveyed the drab motel room,
and felt a curious calmness. I was near the end of

my brief odyssey in a world that had no use for me, nor I for it.

Morning sunlight reflected on the snow and created the illusion of warmth. Everything is a matter of sensation and perception.

I showered, then tried the phone number listed for Wendy Pouldice. A recording told me that phone lines in the area were down.

I asked the morning clerk about large riverfront homes.

"Pouldice," he said. "North. About a mile up you take your first left after the curve. It's a big white house on the river."

I bought coffee and walked along the side of the road, watching snow buntings flutter into the air as I approached, then settle again in the field behind me. The birds sought last year's corn stubble, and they were successful despite the new inches of snow. I wished that I had been born to this world of farms and forests and few people.

The dirt drive had been plowed. Pine and spruce trees that lined both sides of the road leaned with the weight of snow, creating a quarter-mile tunnel that remained stunningly bright despite the lack of direct sunlight. At the end of the natural corridor, an open field stretched another quarter mile to the white, three-story, New England house.

One car was parked in the circular drive. There were no cars in the garage.

I skirted the porch and approached the French

doors, peering inside to see the psychiatrist, Lucas Frank, crouched beside a body. I removed the gun from my pocket and kicked open the doors. Broken glass and wood slivers sprayed into the room.

As he turned his hand flew automatically to his gun. He saw me and froze.

"Go ahead," I said. "Take out the gun and place it on the floor."

He did as I instructed.

"Move away."

His eyes were vacant, gray, just as they had been at our first encounter.

"You didn't kill him," I said. "He's old kill."

"Did you?" he asked.

I shook my head. "I would have," I said. "You've been tracking me. Someone is ahead of us."

"It looks that way."

"Do you suppose that person is after me, you, or Ms. Pouldice?"

"She would be my first guess. Her study is a shambles."

"Someone else believes she is not what she seems, that she knows more than she says. Why did you come here?"

"To talk with her."

"To seek her assistance in finding me," I said. "She would have told you nothing."

"That's pretty much what she's been telling me."

"How foolish of her," I said. "There are no cars in the garage. Is the Explorer yours?"

He nodded.

I gazed at Pouldice's paintings, the grand piano, a silver candelabra. "She accumulated wealth at my sister's expense," I said.

"Did Fremont talk before you killed him?"

"He was easily persuaded."

"I made the connection to Fremont through the Theresa Stallings case. How did you do it?"

"I saw him on TV."

"What about Fremont and Pouldice?"

"High school friends in North Carolina."

"You witnessed what happened the day your sister disappeared," he said.

I studied his eyes. "Did you know that there is only a single moment of consciousness when past, present, and future are one?"

"I've heard that," he said. "It is the moment before we die."

"Perhaps it's time that you and I talk," I told him. "You drive. We're going back to Boston."

CHAPTER 31

SUNLIGHT GLISTENED ON THE SNOW-covered pines lining the interstate. A clear cold blue sky heightened the impression that I was driving through a postcard.

This photo had a flaw.

A giant who might slip into a delusional state at any moment sat in the passenger seat with a gun resting on his lap. I had little choice but to be content with my role of chauffeur.

Zrbny wanted to talk, and I listened.

I hoped that he did not bump against one of his crazy buttons, and that I did not nudge him in that direction. I have been in situations where tipping over my subject was essential to getting the information I wanted. This was not one of them.

"When I was ten my sister Levana took me to see tigers in the zoo," he said. "They are magnificent animals. They lay on rocks licking their paws and stretching like house cats. We can't see the ferocity, but we know it's there. I felt the energy. They are . . . potential. They never lose their desire to attack and rip and kill. The zoo attendants toss them bloody meat and the tigers tear at it. If they were in the wild, it would be different. They would shred the attendants. Tigers are the supreme predators. Instinct allows little room for moral judgment."

Zrbny's delivery was flat. He spoke slowly, as if deliberating briefly between sentences.

"I've never been to New York," he said, "but I could find my way around the city. San Francisco, New Orleans, Washington, D.C., and the same is true of Boston. I was fourteen when they locked me up, but I learned from TV. Internet maps were helpful, but I wanted to know what places looked like. If I were to walk on Third Avenue in New York and look up at the buildings, I'd want to be able to recognize landmarks, to know where I was."

"I got lost in Chicago one time," I said. "I thought I knew the city. I didn't. The traffic cop I asked for directions didn't know it either."

Zrbny smiled. "I watched TV before they locked me up," he said, "but I didn't study it. It was just on, and I was aware of it. At my first court hearing, a psychiatrist said that TV violence had influenced me, contributed to my homicidal behavior. I think she was there to help me, but what she said was not true. I imagine there are people who are infatuated with televised images of shootings, stabbings, beatings, whether they are drama or news footage, but I don't think the influence TV has is related to content. It's the format, the medium it-self, and the nature of this country and the people who live here."

Felix Zrbny positioned himself as an outsider. He talked about the world as a place he observed but did not participate in.

"I don't know what it's like for other people who kill," he said. "I can speak only for myself. There have been arguments favoring televised execu-tions. That would not be a deterrent. When you know what you must do, you do it. When they had public executions in England, the rate of death-penalty crimes immediately increased. The hang-ings were exciters, not deterrents."

Zrbny gazed at the snow-covered hills. "TV asks you to sit passively and to receive its entertainment and its commercial messages. We've been trained to be acquisitive, to want things we never knew ex-isted and have no use for. We've always been good at violence, but never with the frequency and fe-rocity of the last fifty years. That's where format comes in. While you sit watching, you're hit with a never-ending barrage of rapid-fire images that de-stroy any attention span you might have. Any de-sire to think, to consider, to reason, is replaced with a need for excitation. The insidious beauty of it is that you don't know what's happening. You run out and buy a particular brand of soda or beer and wait for your erection to arrive. That might seem innocuous enough, but then you have to run farther and faster to find the pleasure you've been told you're entitled to. Then it hits you. It's not the beer or the soft drink you want. It's the woman caressing the bottle."

"Did you view it this way at fourteen?" I asked.

"It was background noise then. When my father watched his sitcoms, sometimes I looked at them. It was different for him. His world had died and he was passing time until it was his turn to be among the dead. He laughed with the laugh track."

Many of Zrbny's thought processes and notions were paranoid, but his was a reality-based paranoia. TV can exist only when it sells product. To that end, the medium must influence behavior.

"People search for images of themselves," he continued. "They crave the resonance that comes with discovering their reflections on the screen. They want to hear and see what they already believe to be true. It happens so fast that they forget the time when they could read, hold a coherent thought, and express themselves in complete sentences."

"How did you avoid the trap?"

"I told you. I studied TV. I was the aggressor, not the passive victim. Did you watch the Simpson trial?"

My daughter Lane had sent me tapes of key testimony. "Some," I said.

"I watched it with a friend. Do you think that

Lance Ito was influenced by the presence of the camera in the courtroom?"

"I have heard that criticism of the judge, but not that it affected his rulings."

"His demeanor," Zrbny said. "Marcia Clarke was oblivious at first. She was uninteresting, all sharp edges. Then she became aware of her celebrity. She had her hair done, wore clothes that were less severe, softer colors, feminine. She smiled more often. When someone complimented her on her hairstyle, she told the person to get a life. She didn't know that she was no longer a prosecutor. She had no idea that she had become an actor in a drama. The dead were no longer relevant to the proceedings. The trial had developed a theatrical life of its own. DNA had nothing to do with the case outcome. Few of the witnesses mattered. Kato Kaelin is memorable because he was media-savvy. Clarke had the power of the state of California, but Kato was charismatic. Point to Kaelin. No one remembers the name of the limo driver. His testimony was important, but he had no rerun potential. One person in that courtroom fully understood how to play the media."

"Johnnie Cochran," I said.

"It's obvious, isn't it? What shaped public opinion had nothing to do with evidence. The trial was theater and Cochran was Olivier."

"What about Simpson?"

"All he had to do was struggle to pull on a glove. He was probably disappointed that his role was minor, but he played it well. I used to watch TV docudramas with my friend. After a while they all seemed the same. The content was similar. The format was identical. At nine P.M., without a commercial break, the network slips into opening scenes and credits. They load the first twenty minutes with story essentials and something to hook the audience, some bit of soft pornography or violence. After that, the commercials come like automatic weapons fire. The story is irrelevant until ten P.M., when you discover a plot complication. The network takes a major break for sales, and the script coasts into meaningless drivel. The made-for-TV movie is a homogenized morality play. The good guys always win. Justice is served. We all live happily ever after. Have you ever noticed how they have a voice-over preview of the late news while the minor credits are scrolling?"

"I don't watch much TV, but I have noticed that."

"Sometimes it's a bit confusing. The news is like a series of mini-dramas. Bombs and missiles and guns and knives, then break for the commercial message. There really isn't any morality. There are collective points of view, beliefs, thou-shalt-nots. TV reflects how this country wants to see itself. All the scrubbed white faces selling product and promises. People want to think of themselves as moral. They are right with the world only when they buy, not when they attend church."

Zrbny shrugged and gazed out the window. "They consume. They are compliant. Some of them even register to vote. Then maybe they cross themselves and kneel."

"What about you?"

"I don't fit in your world," he said. "I am glad that I don't. There was a time when I thought I was pretty much like everybody else, but nobody thought I was like them. For a while I resented being excluded. I brooded about it. Then I realized that living at the slender end of the bell curve is not a bad thing."

Zrbny suddenly went silent. I glanced at him and saw what I had seen on Severance's video of their session. His eyes were locked on something far in the distance, something only he could see. He was erect, rigid, motionless.

"When I got to the hospital, they badgered me about feelings," Zrbny said, with the same flat delivery. "They said that I lacked the capacity to care for another person."

He slammed his fist against the dash and buckled it. Plastic cracked and snapped, fragments of vinyl flew through the car. Zrbny's violence was sudden, totally unexpected, and unaccompanied by even the slightest hint of anger.

"I cared about my sister," he said. "She needed the time to study, to make high scores for her scholarship, so I washed the dishes, did her laundry and mine, took care of the bed linen, cleaned the house. When Levana was unhappy, I cried with her. I knew her thoughts and she knew mine."

Zrbny slammed the dash a second time, crushing it. "If feeling love is believing that someone else's life is more important than your own, then I loved my sister and she loved me. I did feel. Then it stopped."

"When she was abducted."

He nodded.

"And the world had to pay?" I asked.

"Not the world. People want a simple picture of the killer—a hulking, drooling, slobbering primitive who is totally insane, incapable of reasoning, and who runs slashing through the city at night. They want to execute him or lock him away forever."

"Some people paid," I said.

"It wasn't like that."

"What was it like?"

Zrbny sat in silence. "Levana would not have wanted me to hurt anyone," he said finally. "Sable asked me when I planned to shoot someone. She didn't want me to shoot Mr. Guzman."

"The man who has the store at the Towers."

He nodded. "He is a kind man. He is abused and insulted but still he smiles, listens to his music, and invites others to listen. He gave me flowers to take to Sable."

I remembered the flowers Sable Bannon grabbed as we walked to the door and to her death.

"I would like these things to matter," Zrbny said. "They don't. This world moves too fast for kindness to matter."

"You saw Fremont take your sister," I said.

Zrbny said nothing.

"You couldn't help her."

"It doesn't matter anymore," he said with a sigh. "Whatever I might have felt I no longer feel. I watched the world for fifteen years and was still startled when I stepped back into it. I saw a man stop on the sidewalk, snow blowing around him, and piss into the gutter. There were not many pedestrians, but there were some. They don't show homeless men relieving themselves on TV. Three kids stood outside Children's Hospital with a large boom box blasting at top volume. They were near a sign reminding passersby that this was a hospital zone and asking them to please be quiet. The three kids were a blend of baggy pants, oversized Chicago Bulls jackets, earrings, and untied basketball shoes, listening to music whose only discernible lyrics were 'fucker' and 'motherfucker.' They tried to bum money and when they were refused they called the people entering and leaving the hospital 'fuckers' and 'motherfuckers.'"

"Did they ask you for money?"

"They looked at me," he said. "Then they looked away. I watched people. It was a novelty for me. I thought I had been launched into a city in mourning. So many people wear black. Trench coats and broad hats for the men; pants and sweaters and jackets for the women. Is this fashion, or an expression of mood? Have you noticed everyone wearing packs? They have little ones strapped to their waists and big ones on their backs filled with their gear."

Zrbny turned to look at me. "What is that gear, that stuff they carry with them at all times? A credit card doesn't take up much space. A change of shoes, perhaps? Weapons? What is in those packs? If Levana were alive, if I had killed no one, if we had completed our education and entered professions, would we too have become pack-carrying rats scurrying through the subway?"

He turned again and watched the highway ahead.

"Perhaps I am insane," Zrbny said. "So is this world."

As we approached the city, he gave directions like someone who had spent his life prowling the streets. He knew the shortcuts, the best routes to avoid traffic. I did not have to ask. He had seen it on TV.

"There are many questions I would like to ask you," I said.

"I will get out in Brookline Village," he said. "When I do, you will drive away. Tomorrow morning at eleven, go to the Public Garden and enter from Arlington Street. When you reach the third bench on your left, sit down and stay there. When I arrive, I'll give you my gun and answer your questions. Then you can turn me over to the police."

I did not understand, but I was in no position to demand an explanation. I stopped at a streetlight and Zrbny stepped from the car.

"I have no desire to kill you," he said. "You tried to help Sable."

With that, he slammed the door, wound his way through traffic, and disappeared between two buildings.

CHAPTER 32

I WAITED UNTIL LAST LIGHT, THEN WALKED
into Ravenwood.

As I approached the crest of the hill, I saw a police cruiser's light bar. The cops had parked there,
waiting for me to come home.

"Tomorrow," I muttered. "Not now."

I climbed over a snowbank and struggled through
the drifts into the woods. I moved parallel to Ridge
Road, eventually intersecting the old and familiar
path. The big rock squatted downhill on my left. To
my right, where a gray birch and an oak had marked
my entrance to the dungeons, pines, poplar, and
sumac claimed the terrain.

I studied angles and distances, then crashed into
the undergrowth and dug through the snow and a
fifteen-year accumulation of matted leaves and pine
needles. My fingers throbbed with freezing pain as I
grasped the loop handle and yanked open the iron
door.

The odor of dampness and dirt and rot spilled on
warm air from the hole in the earth. I crawled for-

ward on my stomach, crouched, and turned when I reached the five-foot concrete drainage pipe. I slithered back and pulled the door into place.

My hands ached as I crept the hundred yards through the black, dank conduit, and finally stood in the cistern beneath the dungeons. I groped at the rough walls until I found the iron ladder, still securely bolted in place, and climbed.

The fort was a work of genius—simple in function, complex in design. Its many levels, corridors, and cells were like an animal's arteries and veins. There were no breaks, no disruptions in space. However disguised it might be, there was only continuity.

At the top of the ladder, I stepped into what I had always called the great room, a sixty- by forty-foot space with a fifteen-foot ceiling and a single doorway. I felt the spaciousness; I could not see it. As a child—and now—I imagined knights or generals sitting at an immense hardwood table drinking wine from silver goblets or whiskey from the bottle.

Even in the coldest winters, I had never known the temperature in the dungeons to dip below fifty degrees. The earth's warmth spread through the maze of corridors, insulated by concrete walls that were six inches thick.

I stepped through the doorway and into the main tunnel. Despite my knowledge of the place, I moved slowly, wary of watery pits that had opened in my absence.

To be alone in impenetrable darkness is not to be

deprived of sensation. Through the years of my childhood, I was more comfortable in these halls than I was in my home. Other kids were warned away by parents or police. My mother and father were oblivious to the fort's existence.

The cops who patrolled the hill never caught me. If they arrived as I wound my way through the field, I kept going, knowing they would not follow. If they sat and waited, I retreated to the path and used the entrance only I knew.

I found the narrow corridor that I wanted and turned to my left. The squeak and scratch of rats scuttling ahead of me echoed in the long hall. The familiar, shit-sweet stench of decomposing flesh wafted on the air.

Bats fluttered past my head. I could not see them, but I heard and felt their presence.

Thirty yards in I discovered the cell. I groped in the darkness and found the wood that I had carried to the room and stacked fifteen years earlier. Despite rot, enough fragments of boards and tree branches remained intact for me to start a small fire. I found my box of wooden matches still sealed in plastic and ignited the first few scraps of tinder.

Small flames spread from the half dozen matches to the wood shavings and splinters and licked at the pine sticks and small boards. There was little light at first, but as the fire caught and I felt its warmth on my hands, I gazed beyond the flames at my sister Levana's skull.

CHAPTER 33

"I'VE MADE A FRIEND FOR LIFE," I announced to Bolton, collapsing into the chair in front of his desk.

He leaned back and waited.

"I drove Felix Zrbny back from Pouldice's place in New Hampshire."

"And?"

"He wanted out in Brookline Village. I didn't argue with him because he had a gun aimed at me."

"Where did he go?"

I shrugged. "He disappeared into an alley."

Bolton pushed his hand through his hair and sighed.

"Braverman's dead," I said. "Felix and I agree that neither of us killed him. Pouldice wasn't around. Your boot gun is at the scene."

Bolton winced. "Did you notify the New Hampshire authorities?"

"Not with a gun pointed at me."

"I'll call them."

"The study was trashed. Somebody went looking for something."

"What did Zrbny have to say?"

"Let me make sure I get this right," I said, gazing at the ceiling. "He has studied TV for fifteen years, it sucks and so does the world."

"That's it?"

"He wants to talk to me again tomorrow at the Public Garden. He said he would answer my questions then. He would like a half hour, then you can arrest him."

I expected Bolton to come rocketing out of his chair. He did not. He cocked his head to the right.

"How do you know he didn't kill Braverman?"

"I don't know it. Braverman had been dead for a couple of hours. Zrbny's entrance at the house impressed me as his first."

"Pouldice?"

"No sign of her."

"Would she kill Braverman?"

"She wouldn't shoot it out with him. His gun had been fired. He had a half-inch hole in his forehead, not inflicted from close range. Someone is a good or lucky shot."

"I don't get it."

"Zrbny didn't say why he went up there. We know he was after Pouldice. Were they going to plan his TV career? Doubtful. He's made the connection between Vigil and BTT, says Fremont and Pouldice were high school chums in North Carolina. I figure he planned to break her neck like he's doing to half the population. Why is he meeting me tomorrow to give himself up? I don't know, Ray."

"You're supposed to know more than everything," Bolton said.

"You're not paying me enough. Maybe he plans to wrap up his business tonight."

"Kill Pouldice?"

"I doubt that he could find her."

Bolton sat in silence.

"What about Waycross?" I asked.

He shook his head. "When we couldn't find him, I went to the monastery on Humboldt Avenue. He didn't withdraw from the Brotherhood. When the news broke about Zrbny petitioning for release, the Brothers suspected that Waycross was drinking. They gave him a couple of breaks, then asked him to leave."

Bolton swiveled in his chair and gazed out the window.

"Did they have any idea where he might be?" I asked.

"Someone will find him on the streets," he said. "Maybe he'll be alive, maybe not."

After a pause, Bolton said, "You're lucky Zrbny didn't feed you to the bears. We wait until morning?"

I shrugged. "He's calling the shots," I said.

"What about Pouldice? She isn't at the Towers. Her office hasn't heard from her."

"She's a survivor," I said, pushing myself from the chair. "She'll show up, but not before Zrbny is in custody."

"Where are you headed now?" Bolton asked.

"The psych unit. I want to have another talk with Ben Moffatt."

MOFFATT MET ME IN THE LOBBY.

"Nelson must have had a tune-up," I said, watching my bathrobed man cruise the waiting area.

"He says he feels much better," Moffatt said with a smile.

As I described my encounter with Zrbny, Moffatt nodded. "When he aimed the gun at me," he said, "I knew he wouldn't shoot me. I also knew that I couldn't push him."

I had felt the same way. "He mentioned watching the Simpson trial with a friend," I said.

"Ralph Amsden," Moffatt said quickly. "He's been here since Lyndon Johnson was in the White House. Ralph and Felix were our very own odd couple. Ralph's a fussy little guy, great mechanic, worked on ships' boilers in the navy and pretty much keeps our ancient steam furnace operational. Felix was the new giant on the block, quiet, private, laid-back."

"May I talk with Mr. Amsden?" I asked.

"Ralph hasn't had a visitor since his sister died years ago. He'll talk to you, but don't expect him to tell you anything about Felix."

Moffatt led me into a locked corridor and down a flight of stairs. "This is a secure area," he said, "but it's for maintenance and laundry. The kitchen is down here, too. Meals go to the wards on hand trucks."

Hospital routines had not changed much from when I did my psychiatric residency decades earlier. The acrid smell of bleach mingled with the scent of corned beef hash.

"Ralph lives in a room near the furnace," Moffatt explained. "He hasn't had an assigned therapist in years. He's content with his privacy, and the administration is happy to leave him alone."

Moffatt tapped on an open door. "Ralph? You in there?"

"Hey, Ben. Jesus. Yeah. Come in."

Amsden, the man I had watched push his laundry cart through the lobby on my previous visit, sat on a cot reading the Bible.

"Got a visitor who'd like to ask you some questions," Ben said. "This is Dr. Frank."

He bookmarked and closed his Bible. "Jesus. I seen you on TV."

"Sometimes the camera can't be avoided," I said.

Amsden barked a dry laugh.

"This morning I drove from New Hampshire with your friend Felix."

"Felix was in New Hampshire? Jesus. What was he doing there? I was up there one time. Don't remember why."

"I had hoped that you might have some idea why he went there, and where he'd be now. I dropped him off in Brookline Village."

Amsden considered the information. "If I knew, and if I told you, you still couldn't find him. When he's ready to come in, he'll come in."

"He wants to meet me tomorrow morning," I said.

The old man nodded. "If Felix said that, he'll be there."

"I don't want anyone else to get hurt."

"You can't stop it," Amsden said. "Jesus. One way or another, Felix will do what he needs to do. I had friends when I was in the service. He's the only friend I had since. If I knew something, I still wouldn't tell you."

"I appreciate your honesty," I said.

I scanned Ralph Amsden's small corner of the world, dimly aware of his conversation with Ben Moffatt. A crucifix complemented his Bible. He had crates for furniture, a table, a rickety chair, and a TV that qualified for antique status. I crossed the room and gazed at his only window, a ground-level tilt window covered outside by a steel grate. The gray paint around the window was chipped, and the accumulation of dust on the sill had recently been disturbed. The grate appeared secure, but the screw holes in the frame were empty.

"There's another consideration," I said without turning from the window. "I doubt that you would want to see your friend shot down by police."

"Jesus, no," he said, an edge of panic creeping into his voice.

"He killed a deputy sheriff," I continued. "Cops hate cop killers."

"He said he'll meet you tomorrow," Amsden protested. "Felix doesn't lie."

"What if a police officer stumbles across him tonight?" I asked, turning to survey three low storage lofts, sheets of plywood supported by two-by-fours.

"The cops won't find Felix. They can't. Jesus. Felix is very smart."

I nodded as I walked to the loft on my far right and placed my hand on a box of toilet tissue. "On the off chance that they did find him, he couldn't visit with you again, could he?"

"Those crates ain't up there sturdy," he said with a tremor in his voice.

I faced Amsden and stared at his eyes. He shifted his glance.

"May I call you Ralph?" I asked.

He did not answer.

"You have no plans to leave here, Ralph, do you?"

"No. Jesus. I wouldn't know what to do out there."

I waited several moments. "Ralph?"

"Felix is with his sister. Leave him be. If you go in there after him, everybody gets hurt. Jesus."

"In where?"

He shot a glance at the window. "The dungeons."

"The old fort at Ravenwood?"

He nodded curtly.

"That's the place I told you about," Moffatt said.

"Felix won't let you take him away from his sister," Amsden said.

MOFFATT ESCORTED ME BACK THROUGH THE corridors to the lobby. "You threatened him," he said, "but I'll be damned if I know how you did it."

"I suggest that you get one of your maintenance people to do a routine check on basement window security," I told Moffatt. "I think Ralph has been offering his Lincoln bedroom to guests."

AS I WALKED TO MY CAR, I EXPECTED TO run into Danny Kirkland. "Conditioned response," I muttered.

His office was his apartment on Beacon Street. Perhaps it was time to hear his theory.

The brownstone, an impossible homer from Fenway Park, was ten blocks east of my old office. There were six apartments, Kirkland lived on the top floor, and the street door required no key. The drawback was the walk up three flights.

I pounded on his door. It did not open, but the door behind me did.

"You looking for Danny?" a young woman asked.

"I thought I might catch him in."

She shook her head. "I think he's dead. Someone should call the cops."

"Why do you think he's dead?"

"I heard a gunshot. I don't have a phone or I would've called. I was afraid to open the door. Everybody else in the building works days. I work nights. There was the bang, then I heard the door click shut and the guy go down the stairs. I knew you weren't him coming back. He's much bigger."

I wedged my knife between the hollow door and the jamb, then nudged the door with my foot. It swung open.

"Are you a cop?" she asked.

"I work with the police. Is there a public phone nearby?"

"On the corner."

I handed her Bolton's card. "Please call him. Tell him to get over here."

She took the card, vanished into her apartment, reappeared in a parka, and ran down the stairs.

I stepped into Kirkland's kitchenette. He had piled dishes in the sink, Kmart's blue light specials encrusted with tomato sauce and bits of what might have been ground beef. Empty Ragu jars littered the counter.

I moved to the right, into the dining-living area. A sofa bed was open, its stained gray sheets emitting a lethal smell. I avoided a coffee table strewn with empty beer cans and overfilled ashtrays. Kirkland lay on the floor between the table and bed, his nose and jaw broken, one eye closed, one oddly open. A single, large-caliber shot to the head had ended his pain.

I retreated around the table and gazed into the room Kirkland used for an office. The space was a blizzard of discarded files, computer disks, notebooks, and photographs.

Ray Bolton appeared in the doorway.

"J-Cubed was right about your aftershave," I said. "It precedes you."

"Saves the trouble of waiting to be announced."

"Looks like someone else had an interest in Kirkland's theories," I said.

"Think they got what they came after?"

"If he had it, he would have given it up when he saw the gun."

"This could have nothing to do with Zrbny," Bolton said. "Kirkland wasn't Mr. Popular."

"This shit looks like Pouldice's study," I said. "Braverman caught the big one with his head; so did Danny. You know how I feel about coincidence."

CHAPTER 34

THE SMALL FIRE BURNED STEADILY.

Two friends had joined Levana since my last visit. One, like my sister, was a disarrayed pile of bones. The second accounted for the lingering odor of decomposition. She had been in the dungeons for only a few months.

My hands and fingers had warmed and I could flex them. I removed the matches from the plastic bag, neatly folded the scraps of Levana's clothing that remained, and placed them in the bag. I lifted her skull from the bone pile and rested it on the soft clothes. Then I resealed the bag.

When I was twelve and walked through the tunnels in search of my sister, I found her dead, her body punctured fifty-one times. I touched each wound as I counted, wishing that I could force the blood back into her body. I stayed with her that night, and told my father that I had wandered through Ravenwood searching for Levana. I kissed her forehead, held her hand, and wept for the last time in my life.

I waited two years to hear her voice, to hear my

lady of sorrow. Levana was the keeper of all tears and sighs, and all darkness inhered in her.

I picked up my plastic bag and moved through the narrow hall to the main corridor and back to the great room. It was there that I heard the thrum of a helicopter and felt its steady pounding overhead.

I entered the north tunnel and walked fifty yards to the circular iron stairway that led to the top of the lookout tower. I climbed slowly, testing the strength of the support pins driven into the stone wall a hundred years earlier. The rhythmic throb grew louder as I neared the observation area, and became deafening when I stepped out against the retaining wall. A police helicopter hovered at eye level, churning ice crystals and frigid air against my face, illuminating the field below with its halogen spotlights.

Heavily armed and armored tactical officers jogged across the field on compact aluminum snowshoes. They were prepared. The terrain would not swallow them, but the dungeons would.

I descended the stairs, wound my way back to the great room, and climbed down the ladder into the cistern. Above me, boots clattered on the concrete, lights arced and flashed briefly. I waited until I heard an officer's startled shout followed by radio chatter.

I wound the top of the plastic bag around my hand and crawled through the conduit, dimly aware of the continuing noise behind me. Eventually all sound faded except the distant helicopter blades whipping the air.

CHAPTER 35

I SHOWERED, THEN LINGERED OVER A LONG breakfast in the hotel restaurant. One local paper had caught up with ZRBNY: FOUR DEAD IN JAMAICA PLAIN BAR. Another paper reported the SLAUGHTER ON HUNTINGTON AVENUE. Riddle's was not on Huntington, nor was it remotely near a Tenth Avenue, and even if Richard Rodgers were alive I doubted he would do the score. Danny Kirkland made page two. There was no mention of the head in the hall outside my door.

"BTT is still covering the bloodbath in Boston," Bolton said as he joined me.

He had grabbed a *New York Times* on his way in.

"Same as the *Globe*," I muttered.

"What?"

"The *Times* owns the *Globe*."

"No way."

I shrugged.

"Lucas, *The New York Times* does not own *The Boston Globe*."

"That fact seems to come as a shock to most people," I said. "I thought I'd have to get Lane adult diapers when I told her. What time is it?"

"When are you gonna get a watch?"

"Never wore one in my life. Lane keeps giving them to me, and I keep shoving them in drawers. I refuse to be a slave to time."

"Then why are you asking me?"

"Never mind," I said, flipping open Hearst's Boston effort.

"Seven-fifteen."

"Plenty of time."

Bolton ordered ham and eggs. "Two officers injured last night," he announced. "Like you said, no Zrbny."

"I want my half hour with him," I said.

"Lucas . . ."

"I'm the bait. It's my call."

"Suppose he walks in there and blows off your head."

"He won't," I said, sounding more confident than I felt.

Bolton described how he would deploy his officers around the Public Garden. "The chopper will be to the east," he said, "at a thousand feet above the Park Street Underground. There will be a marksman on a roof behind you, and another on Boylston Street."

"Did Pouldice survive the night?"

"She left a message. Says she's coming in this afternoon, that she had nothing to do with Braverman. She heard shots and ran."

"I have to be in the Public Garden at eleven," I said, pushing aside the newspaper.

"You trust Zrbny, don't you?"

"More than I trust *The New York Times*. Their management doesn't like Noam Chomsky. I do."

"When I've had my coffee, I'll ask who he is," he said. "I know there's no point trying to talk you out of—"

"None," I said.

"I was going to suggest that I—"

"No."

"—walk in with you."

I grabbed the newspaper and read *Dilbert*.

"You get like this when you're nervous," he said.

I looked up from the comics. "Astute," I said. "I'd be a damn fool to not be nervous."

"Why do you keep doing stuff like this? Let me do my job."

I slapped down the comics. "When Zrbny reenters the system, the behavioral entrepreneurs with their questionnaires will be the only people who get to talk to him. Then there will be a spate of books, and a herd of former FBI something-or-others will hit the talk show circuit. They won't know shit about Felix Zrbny, but they'll toss labels like rice at a wedding, coin clever descriptive phrases, and borrow money against their royalty checks. You will be as locked out as everyone else while the public is led to believe crap that is more the product of a theorist's ego than it is of Zrbny's psyche." I leaned across the table. "Ray, haven't we had this discussion before?"

"Twenty-five years ago," he said with a wry smile. "In your kitchen."

WHILE BLITHELY WALTZING THROUGH MY conversation with Bolton, I had managed to distance any sense of the reality of what my morning entailed. But as I emerged from the subway at the corner of Arlington and Boylston Streets, that reality hit me like an eighteen-wheeler.

I walked to meet a killer, alone, on a park bench in the Boston Public Garden. No swan boats; no cops for a half hour. Before panic got its foothold, I told myself that if Felix Zrbny wanted me dead, I would be dead. He had held a gun on me twice, and one of those times for nearly three hours.

Whenever I think about dying, I am comforted by the notion that there is nothing beyond life. I don't want to deal with clouds and harps and angels, or demons and fires and pitchforks. I much prefer to simply hop on the Oblivion Express and have done with it.

Also, despite Zrbny's gift of Fremont's head, I did not think he had summoned me to practice his precision anatomical work.

Perhaps Zrbny could not help himself. Maybe he knew that, and maybe there were enough circuits still clicking upstairs for him to realize that he had arrived at the end of the line. He had created a stir that would remain in the media for weeks, certain to be followed by a televised trial on BTT.

The city slowly returned to life. Trucks spewed diesel fumes. Automobile traffic strained more than usual to stop at lights. Cars slid into intersections, creating more than the customary din of bumper crunches.

I entered the park and walked through the chill, late-morning air. A woman strolled hand-in-hand with her daughter. An old man in tattered tweed fed cracked corn to the pigeons. A young couple— I thought one male and one female—shared a joint and stared at the barren trees, the nearly frozen pond. The pond probably would not quite freeze; there was enough bacterial action going on in there to generate defensive heat.

I looked back at the gate and counted benches. The man in tweed and white chin stubble tending the rock doves occupied number three on the left.

"You the doc?" he asked.

He looked like he had just tossed back his cardboard quilt for the day. "Lucas Frank," I said. "I'm supposed to meet a man here."

"Great big guy."

I nodded.

He stood. "You get the seat and the bag of corn. I'm gonna get some breakfast."

He walked toward Boylston Street.

"That's it?"

"I'm hungry," he shouted, and quickened his pace.

The young couple—two men? two women?—on the next bench soared somewhere above the pond. Pigeons murmured, flurried a foot in the air, then settled back on the corn, their bobbing heads allowing them to visualize depth.

"You're a fucking miracle of nature," I muttered to the birds. "Raccoons wash their food before they eat it. You shit on yours."

The police helicopter hummed in the distance, a black dot against a blue sky.

Zrbny entered the Public Garden from Beacon Street. He moved easily through a gaggle of tourists. No heads turned.

After three days of uninterrupted TV coverage, his was probably the most famous face in Boston. According to BTT, the city was under siege, its residents in a state of panic. Folks probably were terrified, I thought, but they were not observant. No one pointed, screamed, fainted, or dove into the pond.

Zrbny sat next to me on the bench and placed a plastic garbage bag on the pavement between his feet. "Do you know what catgut is?" he asked.

I looked at him. "Fishing line," I said. "It's

single-strand, and strong. I used it mackerel fishing when I was a kid."

"Look at my right index finger."

He sat rigidly, as he had in his session with Randy Severance, his hands resting on his thighs. There was a monofilament loop secured to his finger.

"That strand extends up my sleeve," he said, "and attaches to the trigger on a nine-millimeter handgun that is secured to my chest and aimed at you. The action is already engaged. If I flinch, the gun fires. If the man on the roof behind us shoots, we both die."

Zrbny's delivery was the same deliberate monotone I had registered on our drive from New Hampshire. Despite the chill, sweat beaded on the back of my neck.

"What's in the bag?" I asked.

"My sister."

Zrbny was near the edge, teetering in a land where only he knew the terrain.

"You have questions," he said.

As the midday break approached, a small army of office workers scurried past on the wet pavement. Bolton's nightmare had come true. He wanted us out of the Garden before the lunch rush.

I considered Zrbny's preference for chronological accounts. Wherever I began, I would have to be content with his unfolding of events. I could not risk disrupting his flow, and I had little time.

"You were eligible for release four years ago," I said.

"I wouldn't have bothered. It was Wendy's idea. She wanted my story. I wanted to know who killed my sister. She had been investigating Levana's disappearance for years."

I took advantage of the pause, hoping that my statement did not require Zrbny to make any cerebral adjustments. "You two have known each other for years," I said.

"A few days after Fremont killed my sister, Wendy came to our house. We kept in touch. It was more her idea than mine, but I did call her the day I killed those people."

"I wondered about that."

"It wasn't a secret. No one ever asked me."

"Do you remember what you told her?"

"Of course. I said that Levana had spoken to me, that today was the day. Right here. Right now."

"Neville Waycross interrupted you."

"Does it matter now?"

"I'm curious, only because there are three ladies of sorrow. You had killed three times."

A slight smile creased Zrbny's lips. "You're very good," he said.

"There were more?"

"Continue with your questions."

As Ben Moffatt had said, Zrbny did not lie. He simply did not answer. I gazed into the distance, focusing on the helicopter dot.

"Wendy Pouldice gave you Fremont."

"She could have given him to me sooner. When I saw him, I remembered him."

"What about the courthouse shootings?"

"I didn't know anything about that until the next night."

"Ralph Amsden told you."

Again I saw the hint of a smile.

"Secure his window," Zrbny said, "but don't remove him from his room."

"That's what I think will happen."

Zrbny took a deep breath and slowly exhaled. "The police can't prove any of this," he said. "Wendy is clever, not your average TV airhead. She was impatient, didn't want to wait for the system to release me. She knew I wouldn't agree, so she said nothing and made her arrangements. She also didn't want to be implicated in shooting up a courthouse. I was supposed to know what to do when the shooting started. Maybe I would have. I don't know."

Zrbny could have climbed out Ralph's window anytime. Instead, he had waited for the Commonwealth to free him.

"The accident was . . . an accident," he said, "one of those fortuitous events that no one can plan. What I did was up to me. I liked that. When I walked into Sable's apartment, I thought it was an aquarium shop. I looked at her and I saw my sister."

He pulled his plastic bag onto his lap. "I still haven't heard Levana's voice. I thought I would."

Zrbny gazed at the blue sky. "My sister was not alone," he said. "There are other remains in the dungeons."

I pointed at his bag. "Is that what all of this has been about?"

He remained silent.

Our lunch traffic had evaporated. My stoned androgynes were gone. Cruisers blocked the entrances to the Public Garden, and Ray Bolton approached on the path from Boylston Street. The police helicopter thrummed lower, closing on the pond. Tactical officers scaled the fences and moved through the deep snow.

"Pouldice and Fremont," I said.

Zrbny released the catgut loop on his index finger.

"I told you they were friends. It doesn't matter now."

"You went to New Hampshire to kill her."

"She disappointed me."

"That's it?"

"For now," he said, unzipping his jacket. "You

take the gun. If I remove it, they'll shoot me. I'm not ready to die yet."

BOLTON AND I WATCHED AS OFFICERS searched and shackled Felix Zrbny.

"BTT has a camera crew on the roof," he said, pointing at Boylston Street. "They've also got a parabolic microphone. I don't know how good it is at this distance."

"Sure is a different world, isn't it? I don't think we're any more violent than we ever were. We just get better media coverage."

CHAPTER 36

A GUARD ENTERED THE CORRIDOR AND placed a chair opposite my cell. "Your lawyer's here," he said.

I stood at the bars and waited. The short, stocky man who approached carried a battered briefcase in one hand, an Italian sandwich dripping olive oil in the other. He sat on the chair, dropped the briefcase, and filled his mouth with sandwich.

"Fuckin' good shit," he said. "I'm Hensley Carroll."

His shirt had pulled itself loose from his pants, allowing his belly roll to spill from beneath his undershirt. He wore rubber boots with clips.

"I'm your attorney," he said. "I'm on the court record as representing you, so I gotta see you through the arraignment tomorrow morning. After that, the court will appoint someone else to represent you."

He took another bite from his sandwich. "Okay, I'll do all the talking. Same as tomorrow. We enter a not guilty plea, you get remanded, we're out of there in a half hour tops."

Carroll stared at his fistful of food. "Only problem with these fuckin' things is all my ties look like they just had lube jobs. You're gettin' arraigned for offing the cop, the deputy sheriff, Finneran. Nice guy. Good family. Irish Catholic. Grew up in Jamaica Plain. Anyway, the rest of the shit will come later. You understand? You got any questions?"

He hesitated only a moment. "Aces. I'm outta here."

"Wait."

"Holy shit. He talks."

"Who is paying you?"

"I got paid. What do you care?"

I watched his face as he mouthed his sandwich and sweat beaded on his forehead.

"I got a cashier's check, okay? I don't know who paid me. All I know is I'm on the fuckin' record and I can't get off till after tomorrow. This is a formality, okay? Jesus. I pity the fuckhead who gets this case. He says not guilty, and the D.A. shows an instant replay. If we had the chair, you'd be a crispy critter."

I turned from the bars and stepped to the back of my cell, where I examined the texture of the concrete blocks.

Carroll's footsteps faded in the hall. The lawyer bantered with the guard about the Boston Celtics. Both men swore and laughed, and the steel door slammed.

The silence was a delight.

CHAPTER 37

OUR TABLE WAS AT THE REAR OF JACOB Wirth's. Bolton was on his second dark beer before dinner, and in storytelling mode.

"We'd just gotten the DNA lab up and running," he said. "A couple of department clowns were fussing about whether Albert DeSalvo was the 'Boston Strangler.' They wanted to run tests, make a definitive announcement, but they didn't have anything to test. Jimmy Wheaton, BTT's guy who does 'Talk about Boston,' called. I figured he wanted to discuss the new lab, but the last time I was on that show, Wheaton threw me more than a few curveballs. I made these cards, about the size of business cards, and I printed 'Fuck You' on each one."

"Not very nice, Raymond," I said. "Sounds like something I'd do."

"Listen," he continued. "Jimmy's first question was about the bad blood between some of the cops and the highway department. There was stuff in the *Boston Record*, but that was all I knew about it. Instead of answering the question, I handed him a

card. We were on live. He handled the first one,
skirted the issue, asked me about the lab, then he
landed on the BPD's image. I gave him another
one."

I laughed.

"At the commercial break he said, 'Ray, you're
killing me. What are you doing?' I told him to stop
using me as a straight man, and we were fine for
the last twenty minutes. I got the idea from you."

"Bullshit."

"The hell," Bolton said with a laugh. "You were
my inspiration. Where was it?"

"D.C.," I said.

"That's right. It was back when they had the
seven-second tape delay. You told the guy that
every time he asked a hinky question you were going to say one of those words you aren't supposed
to say on the air. The guy was cocky. He told you
about the tape delay. You said that was fine, you'd
just repeat each word for eight seconds."

"A knowledge of syphilis is not an instruction to
get it," I said, paraphrasing my favorite philoso-
pher of culture, Lenny Bruce.

Our waiter delivered dinner and removed our
empty mugs for refills. Bolton had the German
mixed grill—bratwurst and weisswurst, sauerkraut,
potato salad, and pickled red cabbage. I had ordered Jake's special, knockwurst and bratwurst in
red beer sauce, and the requisite sauerkraut and
potato salad. I stabbed at Bolton's cabbage.

"Waycross should be here," I said.

"He's not a nice drunk," Bolton said. "He was drinking before Shannon died. He didn't drink every day, but when he did, it was uncontrolled. The only department Christmas party he attended, he never left the bar. Shannon was with Louise and me most of the night. When we went home, I guess she danced with a couple of the guys. Neville went after one of them. Remember Steve Winslow?"

I nodded.

"He set Neville down on his butt without too much damage done."

"Except to Neville's ego," I said.

"He took it out on Shannon. Neville can't drink. It's that simple. He was a good cop. When he's sober, he's a likable guy."

"What did he do to Shannon?"

"That night, he slapped her. Couple of months later, he hit her hard enough to knock her down. They ended up in the E.R. He quit drinking. The two of them went to counseling. He slipped a couple of times, but no rough stuff that I know about."

Bolton shrugged. "Then Zrbny."

"When he heard about Zrbny's release petition, he hit the bottle," I said.

"Solace in an old friend," he muttered.

"The Brothers warned him, then tossed him," I mused. "He lied about it."

"Maybe he was embarrassed," Bolton said.

I filched more of Bolton's cabbage.

"The Brothers were willing to support him through treatment," he said. "He didn't want that. They didn't want an aggressive drunk in the monastery."

"Maybe he'll show for the arraignment," I said.

"We can try to talk to him," Bolton said. "Doesn't usually do any good."

"Anything on Braverman?"

"They've got a make and model on the gun that killed him. I'm waiting to hear. We'll test it against Zrbny's."

"Expect it to be the same one that killed Danny Kirkland," I said, "but don't expect it to be Zrbny's."

"You think what's left of Vigil quit BTT and went solo?"

"Whoever dismantled those two offices didn't know where to look for what he was after. I suppose it's possible."

TWO HOURS LATER, I STOOD IN THE HALL outside my hotel room. I studied the carpet, the baseboards, the walls. There was not a speck of evidence that a severed head had been there. I got down on my hands and knees and searched for a stain or a single strand of hair.

"It's like this never happened," I said.

The cleaners had done a thorough job. They had

eradicated the entire event. I wondered if any hotel employees would tell stories about the head in the hall. Doubtful. Everyone is in the business of rewriting the past.

I stood and opened my door. "Guess there wasn't any head there," I said.

I sat on the edge of the bed and wondered if others were as concerned with shaping events to fit their images of themselves.

"We revised the sixties right out of existence," I muttered, clicking the TV remote control to find out what BTT was doing.

They had caught up with the Braverman story. An intruder believed to be Felix Zrbny had shot and killed Wendy Pouldice's personal assistant. Pouldice had narrowly escaped with her life. Police, who concentrated their search for Zrbny in the Boston area, were trying to determine how the mass murderer had eluded the largest dragnet in the city's history since Albert DeSalvo's escape from Bridgewater State Hospital, the reporter said.

"Enough," I said, banging the remote.

I was restless, not ready to sleep. I thumbed through case files, paced the room, and smoked. I grabbed the file that had shaken Neville Waycross. It was a particularly dense set of reports analyzing blood mixtures on Zrbny's knife and at the three scenes.

At two A.M. I fell into bed.

Good morning. I'm Lily Nelson, and this is Boston Trial Television Headline News. Same case, different courthouse. Felix Zrbny will be arraigned this morning in the shooting death of Sheriff's Deputy Michael Finneran. We will be going inside the courtroom in about ten minutes. Right now, let's go to the courthouse steps, where . . .

CHAPTER 38

THREE DEPUTIES STOOD BEHIND ME; TWO deputies led the way into the courtroom. All were armed with stun guns and Mace.

Hensley Carroll sat at the defense table. He had not removed his rubber boots.

"Sit," Carroll said. "Remember what I told you. We do this clean and quick, then we're outta here."

The three deputies took their positions across the front of the court. Two remained directly behind me.

As I expected, a TV camera at the rear observed and recorded everything. Most of the studio audience had taken their seats.

Insects buzzed on a summer day long ago. Water cascaded down the side of the vegetable crisper. I touched my fingers to the liquid and rubbed it on the back of my neck. I had waited fifteen years from that moment when I heard my sister's voice, to this moment, when she spoke to me again.

"Today," my lady of sorrow said, and her soft voice echoed inside, "Today."

I waited patiently for my final scene.

CHAPTER 39

WENDY POULDICE WORE HER GAME FACE TO court. She sported two new bodyguards—African-Americans wearing black suits, dark glasses, and bald pates.

"Your friend Bolton has been making a nuisance of himself," she said.

I waited. I was in no mood for sparring with her.

She surveyed the courtroom, then lowered her voice. "You two are ancients and you don't fucking know it."

I thought of numerous ways to return the jab, but refrained.

"Look at that camera," she continued, pointing at a single TV camera at the courtroom's rear. "That's what the public wants. They don't want summaries. They don't want to hear from Bolton or Captain Newhall. They want to be in the middle of the action as it happens. Disasters are great, but they have a short shelf life. Continuing dramas like Simpson, the JonBenet Ramsay murder, Cary

Stayner in Yosemite, Timothy McVeigh, Theodore Kaczynski . . ."

"That's where the money is," I said.

She smiled. "Get used to it, Lucas. The hero runs for a night. The killer is worth months of prime time."

She turned, and her muscle turned with her. They claimed their second-row, reserved seats.

She's as dangerous as any killer, I thought. *Perhaps more dangerous.*

Bolton slipped into a seat beside me.

"Warrant's on its way," he said.

I nodded. "Our media queen's arrest? Which of her many crimes are you going to nail her with?"

"We'll start with obstruction and go from there. Anything that originates with Zrbny is worthless. We'll need corroboration."

"It's a start," I said, returning my attention to the front. "Boston is in for a treat. Pouldice will play the martyred journalist with aplomb."

"All rise," the bailiff intoned.

"Great theater," I muttered.

Bolton elbowed me.

"In and for the County of Suffolk in the Commonwealth of Massachusetts," the bailiff continued. "The Honorable Nancy Kahn presiding."

As the judge and prosecutor attended to housekeeping matters, I surveyed the packed court.

Reporters scribbled, artists sketched, and the single camera eye recorded the show.

Blood.

Strange how a single word can pop into your head and commandeer your consciousness.

"Something is wrong," I told Bolton.

He waved at me to be quiet.

People want a simple picture of the killer—a hulking, drooling, slobbering, primitive who is totally insane, incapable of reasoning, and who goes slashing through the city at night leaving a sea of blood.

"Ray, Waycross interrupted him," I whispered.

Bolton ignored me.

"*Neville Waycross interrupted you,*" I'd said to Zrbny.

"*Does it matter now?*"

"*I'm curious, only because there are three ladies of sorrow. You killed three times.*"

A slight smile creased Zrbny's lips. "*You're very good,*" he said.

"Not good enough," I muttered.

"Judge Kahn will boot you out of here," Bolton whispered.

I asked Zrbny if he remembered what he had said to Pouldice on that summer day fifteen years earlier.

"*Of course. I said that Levana had spoken to me, that today was the day. Right here. Right now.*"

I had watched him pull what was left of his sister onto his lap.

"I still haven't heard Levana's voice," he said. "I thought I would."

At his trial in 1970, Charles Manson propelled himself over the defense table, landing a few feet in front of Judge Older's bench and falling to one knee. He was quickly subdued.

When Felix Zrbny rose from his seat, his movements were fluid and fast. He turned away from the bench; his target was not the judge. He shoved two deputies aside, planted his foot on the railing, and launched himself into the air. He landed hard on Wendy Pouldice.

Bolton flew from his seat. Four deputies converged on the melee. Pouldice's bodyguards yanked at Zrbny, trying to pull him away. Reporters in adjacent seats moved aside and continued to scribble.

From beneath the human pile, I heard a loud crack and knew immediately that Wendy Pouldice was dead, her neck broken.

Deputies restrained and shackled Zrbny. Judge Kahn ordered the courtroom cleared. Bolton's people secured the area around Pouldice's limp corpse. I stared dumbly as the officers lifted Zrbny to a standing position.

He gazed at me, smiling, and said, "My lady of darkness."

"I don't understand," I said.

• • •

A HALF HOUR LATER, BOLTON AND I STOOD on the sidewalk and watched a county van back into position to collect Felix Zrbny. The crowd, quiet now, moved slowly from the courthouse steps and followed the media army into the alley.

"I don't understand this," a small black man said. "He shoveled for me, cleared the steps, and he wouldn't take a dollar. He shook my hand."

"Eddie," a Hispanic man said, "those flowers in the snow, Felix carried them to Sable."

"He said his name was Felix, but I don't believe he's Felix Zrbny," Eddie concluded.

I turned to Bolton. "If Wendy Pouldice was Zrbny's lady of darkness, what the hell was Shannon Waycross?"

"It doesn't make any sense," Bolton said. "He's crazy."

There were three ladies of sorrow, and Zrbny had killed three times.

Why would Neville Waycross believe that he had interrupted the killer?

"Lucas?"

"Zrbny planned to kill Wendy Pouldice fifteen years ago," I said.

"It's over."

"He always intended to kill her on camera. That was his final scene."

The side door opened. Deputies escorted a shackled Zrbny down a short flight of iron stairs to the waiting van. His face expressionless, his long hair blowing in his face, he gazed into the eerily silent gathering until a man shouted, "She's got a gun."

The crowd retreated as a woman stepped forward and pumped five shots into Felix Zrbny.

He folded and collapsed on the pavement, and cameras caught the action for the evening news.

I saw the woman's profile as deputies restrained and disarmed her. On my first day back in Boston, she had thrown a snowball at me, narrowly missing my head. "You fucking bastard," she had screamed, not knowing her target.

This time she knew who she wanted to take down.

. . . gunshot death of mass murderer Felix Zrbny brings to an end the bloodbath in Boston. Many will argue that it is a fitting end for the man who left an unprecedented trail of carnage in his wake. A concerned citizens' group has already formed a legal defense fund for the woman who emerged from the crowd in the courthouse alley and fired five . . .

CHAPTER 40

MY FLIGHT WAS DELAYED.

I grumbled about it, then found a quiet corner away from the gate area and dipped into my duffel bag in search of George V. Higgins's *Outlaws*. Instead, I dragged out the lab and autopsy files on Shannon Waycross, Gina Radshaw, and Florence Dayle.

I returned to the analysis of blood types and blood mixes, the file that had so distressed Neville Waycross that he vanished, probably wandering the city on one hell of a bender. As I worked backward from the last victim, I found what I expected. Technicians identified two blood types at the Dayle residence, hers and Gina Radshaw's. Transfer, I thought. When Waycross saw Zrbny emerge from the woods, the teenager was blood-soaked and carried a bloodstained knife.

There was no blood mix noted in the Radshaw report, and none in the Waycross report. Zrbny's knife held stains from Dayle and Radshaw, none from Waycross. His clothing—Dayle and Radshaw, no Shannon Waycross.

Zrbny had killed Waycross first, then Radshaw, then Dayle.

"No," I muttered, flipping through the autopsy reports.

I skimmed the external examinations. Radshaw and Dayle were similar: numerous stab wounds, no defensive wounds, no evidence of restraint. Dayle had an appendectomy scar, Radshaw a mole on her stomach.

Shannon Waycross's throat was cut. Traces of an adhesive were found on her ankles, wrists, and near her mouth. On her right hand, two fingernails were broken. Her right cheek and the back of her head bore evidence of blunt-force injury.

No solved homicide ever accounts for all the bits and pieces of evidence and information, but this was glaring. "Someone fucked up," I muttered.

I glanced around for a phone, and that was when I saw Neville Waycross standing in the departure area, surveying the crowd. His hands were stuck deep in his pockets, and he was unsteady on his feet. He was not here to wish me a safe trip, nor would he be inclined to discuss the nuances of evidence. I figured he had primed himself with whiskey and convinced himself that I had to be eliminated. He expected me to discover the inconsistencies in the reports dealing with his wife's death, to realize that he had killed Shannon.

I walked quickly to the opposite wall, where Waycross could not see me. The phones were in the corridor that led to the main terminal. That was out because Waycross had a clear view of the corridor.

I flattened myself against the wall, wondering if Waycross had a gun. He had to pass through metal detectors to get this far. Waycross was an ex-cop. A quick flash of his old ID might get him through.

When I looked out again, Waycross was gone.

There was a bar fifty yards down the corridor where he could grab a bracer and have a place to wait. I walked slowly toward the Budweiser sign, scanning the waiting areas and searching for air-port cops.

Waycross stood at the end of the bar, watching pedestrian traffic enter from the main terminal. Ray Bolton was part of that traffic. I did not have to wonder what he was doing here. He had been waiting for a report on the gun that killed Donald Braverman and Danny Kirkland.

I waved at Bolton, caught his attention, and pointed at the bar where Waycross sat hunched over his shot and beer chaser. Bolton nodded, slowed his pace, and moved to the side of the corridor.

Farther down the corridor the media gang came running—cams, booms, mikes, cables.

Waycross slumped lower over his drinks.

I pointed at the approaching TV storm. Bolton turned and tried to wave them back.

"Detective Bolton," Lily Nelson called.

Waycross raised his head, pushed himself from his stool and away from the bar. His eyes disappeared upward, and he crashed to the floor. He was dead before he got there.

"Not terribly exciting for the late news," I muttered, walking into the bar.

I crouched and felt Waycross's neck for a pulse.

"Did you know that there is a single moment of consciousness when past, present, and future are one?" I asked.

Bolton stood beside me and the cameras rolled.

"Felix Zrbny told me that," I said. "Do you think Waycross caught the triple feature?"

"Dr. Frank," Lily Nelson said.

I looked at Bolton. "Stroke? Heart attack?"

He shrugged. "The gun came back to him. He killed Braverman trying to get to Pouldice. She was a threat to find out that he'd killed Shannon. So was Danny Kirkland. Then Zrbny took out Pouldice, a whacko took out Zrbny, and that left you."

I found the nine-millimeter semiautomatic in Waycross's deep coat pocket and gave it to Bolton. "No one studied the lab reports," I said.

"Not until Waycross did. That's when he panicked. The case was a lock. Zrbny was crazy. He walked out of the woods covered with blood. He was carrying a murder weapon. He attacked a cop. And he never denied anything."

"Shannon fit," I said. "She made a perfect lady of darkness. He watched her out his rear window."

"The log was right. She placed a call two hours after she was supposed to be dead."

TV lights ignited behind us.

"Pouldice lived in Ravenwood," Bolton said. "He could've gotten her whenever the spirit moved him."

"Not on camera."

"Detective Bolton," Lily Nelson said again. "Will you comment on the information we're getting that . . ."

"You clear things with Willy?" Bolton asked.

"I stopped on the way here. Willy needed a little help understanding the advertising potential of bullet holes in his floor and bloodstains in his bathroom. He thanked me for my help."

Bolton looked down at Waycross. "He smells bad."

"Sphincter failed," I said. "You going to retire now?"

Bolton's backup sprinted down the corridor.

"This is Lily Nelson broadcasting live from the departure area at gate . . ."

"I have the paperwork. I'll get to it tonight."

"Have you talked with Mrs. Stallings?"

He nodded. "We took Theresa's remains out of the dungeons. The family can have a funeral now. We've identified one of the other kids."

"My flight is boarding," I said.

"Always good to see you, Lucas."

Bolton's officers cleared the bar.

". . . told that the dead man is former Boston detective Neville Waycross, whose wife . . ."

"You tell her that?" I asked.

Bolton shook his head.

"Fuckin' amazing," I said, shoving my way through the crowd.

ABOUT THE AUTHOR

JOHN PHILPIN is a retired forensic psychologist—an internationally renowned profiler. His advice and opinions on violence and its aftermath have been sought by police, newspaper writers, TV producers, mental health professionals, private investigators, attorneys, and polygraph experts throughout the country. He is the author of *Beyond Murder*, the story of the Gainesville student killings, published by NAL/Dutton in 1994, and *Stalemate*, which tells the true-crime story of a series of child abductions, sexual assaults, and murders in the San Francisco Bay Area. Along with Patricia Sierra, he is the author of *The Prettiest Feathers* and *Tunnel of Night*. He is also the author of the psychological thriller *Dreams in the Key of Blue*. He lives in New England.